Little Annie Smith had just been the victim of an armed bank robbery and was in need of protection. The problem was, she wasn't so little anymore. And Griffin Chase, self-proclaimed guardian, had just watched her throw her bra out the window of his car!

"Are you okay?" Annie asked, once the task was completed.

"I was just wondering about the, uh, this sudden need to divest yourself of, uh…" Griffin stuttered.

She laughed, a delicious, free little giggle that would have reassured him if he'd ever imagined that quiet Annie Smith, the housekeeper's daughter, could make such a sound.

"Oh, Griffin," she said. "I'm just tired of waiting."

Waiting for what?

"From now on, my life is never going to be the same!"

Cold prickles gathered force at the nape of Griffin's neck. Though he'd never considered himself a superstitious man, he suddenly had the terrible feeling *his* life would never be the same, either.…

Dear Reader,

When Patricia Kay was a child, she could be found hiding
somewhere…reading. "Ever since I was old enough to realize
someone wrote books and they didn't just magically appear,
I dreamed of writing," she says. And this month Special
Edition is proud to publish Patricia's twenty-second novel,
The Millionaire and the Mom, the next of the STOCKWELLS
OF TEXAS series. She admits it isn't always easy keeping her
ideas and her writing fresh. What helps, she says, is "nonwriting"
activities, such as singing in her church choir, swimming, taking
long walks, going to the movies and traveling. "Staying well-
rounded keeps me excited about writing," she says.

We have plenty of other fresh stories to offer this month.
After finding herself in the midst of an armed robbery with a
gun to her back in Christie Ridgway's *From This Day Forward,*
Annie Smith vows to chase her dreams…. In the next of A
RANCHING FAMILY series by Victoria Pade, Kate McDermot
returns from Vegas unexpectedly married and with a *Cowboy's
Baby* in her belly! And Sally Tyler Hayes's *Magic in a Jelly Jar*
is what young Luke Morgan hopes for by saving his teeth in a
jelly jar…because he thinks that his dentist is the tooth fairy
and can grant him one wish: a mother! Also, don't miss the
surprising twists in *Her Mysterious Houseguest* by Jane Toombs,
and an exciting forbidden love story with Barbara Benedict's
Solution: Marriage.

At Special Edition, fresh, innovative books are our passion. We
hope you enjoy them all.

Best,

Karen Taylor Richman
Senior Editor

Please address questions and book requests to:
Silhouette Reader Service
U.S.: 3010 Walden Ave., P.O. Box 1325, Buffalo, NY 14269
Canadian: P.O. Box 609, Fort Erie, Ont. L2A 5X3

From This Day Forward

CHRISTIE RIDGWAY

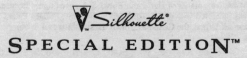

SPECIAL EDITION™

Published by Silhouette Books

America's Publisher of Contemporary Romance

For my big brother, Matt.
Maybe it's not as tasty as my chocolate-chip cookies,
but it is another way of letting you know I love you.

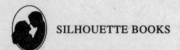 SILHOUETTE BOOKS

ISBN 0-373-24388-X

FROM THIS DAY FORWARD

Copyright © 2001 by Christie Ridgway

Visit Silhouette at www.eHarlequin.com

Printed in U.S.A.

CHRISTIE RIDGWAY

considered herself a writer from that first haiku (about the sound of footsteps in the rain) she wrote in second grade. She became a romance writer in the sixth grade, when she penned a series of love stories starring herself and the teen idol of the time. She turned published author after marrying the love of her life and having two sons.

Now she lives in Southern California, where she writes, wifes and mothers. She prefers not to say which one comes first, but they are all vitally important to her. When she isn't concocting a new story or concocting some way to sneak vegetables into fish sticks and applesauce, she makes time to volunteer in her boys' school. Finally, for her sanity, she always finds a way to curl up with a good book.

You may contact her at P.O. Box 3803, La Mesa, CA 91944.

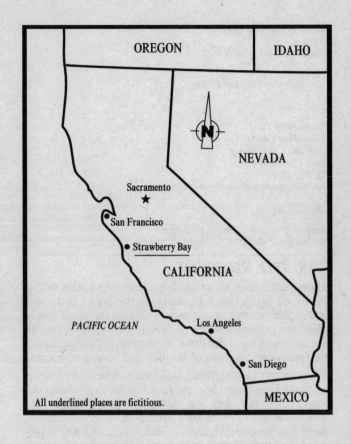

OREGON

IDAHO

N

NEVADA

Sacramento
★

San Francisco

Strawberry Bay

CALIFORNIA

PACIFIC OCEAN

Los Angeles

San Diego

All underlined places are fictitious.

MEXICO

Chapter One

Annie Smith shuffled a half step forward in the long Friday-morning teller-line at her branch of the Strawberry Bay Savings and Loan. Out of the corner of her eye, she saw a harried-looking woman in a silk blouse and business suit speed around the corner from the entry doors, then skid to a halt just millimeters before her nose smacked into Annie's half-turned shoulder.

Annie had been the last in line. Now the harried woman was, and she didn't look very happy about it.

"Unh," the woman grunted in annoyance. "I just hate waiting, don't you?"

Annie quickly murmured a polite noise and spun to face completely forward, unwilling to confess her one guilty secret.

She didn't mind waiting.

Of course, not if it was a line for the ladies' room

or not if she was on her way somewhere important. But as the owner of a small, but growing catering business, and as a twenty-four-year-old—almost twenty-five—single woman, she was a ship under her own steam and her own schedule.

And the fact was, this ship was pretty content to wait her turn. Annie liked watching the other people in line, dreaming up their occupations and lifestyles, amusing herself with their ''Candid Camera''-worthy reactions to the frustrations of using the bank-supplied pens.

Annie tightened her hold on her handful of checks ready for depositing. She'd signed her name and written her account number with her own trusty Bic.

One customer concluded her business, and the line shuffled forward again. Annie shuffled, too, the soles of her discount-store sneakers squeaking against the parquet linoleum. As the satisfied customer strode toward her, Annie noted the silver-dollar-sized hearts dangling from the woman's ears, and her red blouse, pants and high heels. Against the blouse, two more hearts, pink, nodded and bobbed, attached by little springs to a big pin that screamed Happy Valentine's Day! in silver glitter.

Wow. And the fourteenth was still a couple of days away.

Bemused, Annie couldn't help but turn her head as the holiday-happy lady passed her. Which is why she didn't miss seeing the woman don the final touch to her ensemble—a red fuzzy headband that sported two upstanding and overstuffed furry hearts.

It was also why Annie was the first to notice Ronald Reagan enter the bank.

She blinked. She supposed he *could* be in Strawberry Bay, this was California after all, but shouldn't he be accompanied by the Secret Service? And shouldn't *they* be the ones carrying the gun?

The gun.

Just as that started sinking in, the man yelled from behind his mask—the fact that he was wearing one was just starting to sink into Annie's consciousness, too. "Everybody get down!" he shouted. His big, black, scary-looking weapon glinted dully in the light.

Annie discovered she couldn't move. Some people in the line immediately dropped and others shrieked, but Annie was frozen and her voice was, too. Several around her appeared to be just as paralyzed as she.

Then Ronnie aimed the gun at the ceiling and fired.

Annie hit the floor before the first chunks of acoustic ceiling did.

Her cheek pressed against cold linoleum smelling strongly of pine cleaner, Annie tried to make herself as flat as possible. That's what people always did on police shows and "Gunsmoke" reruns. She didn't know exactly why, though, because as the gunman moved her way, she realized that, flat or not, she made an easy target. Her fingernails clawed at the floor, instinctively trying to dig beneath it for cover.

Somewhere close to Annie's right, from her own spot of parquet, the woman who had been standing behind Annie in line moaned.

The terrified sound sucked the last of the air from Annie's lungs. The gunman's shoes came nearer, and when the woman moaned again, Annie kept her eyes on the moving feet and inched her hand in the direction of the sound. The cold, thin fingers of her frightened fellow bank customer clenched hers.

The feet paused.

Annie's heart stopped. The man stood right over her, the gun in his hand feeling like a hundred-pound weight on her back. Stomach roiling, Annie focused on the toes of those black shoes and waited for her life to pass before her eyes.

It didn't happen.

Not until the feet moved on, and she heard the gunman shouting commands to the tellers. It was then, in the few minutes it took for them to follow his directions, that Annie's life replayed in her mind.

Her father's defection when she was four. The move her mother and she made from a tiny apartment to a cottage on the Chase estate when her mother took the position of housekeeper. Public school, cooking school, her mother's retirement. The Chases kind offer to rent Annie the cottage and, finally, the day she opened her own catering business.

Like a winding snake of dominoes, she saw her life as static images that fell, one upon another, leading her to this moment in the Strawberry Bay Savings and Loan. Too swiftly she was dumped back in the present, her cheek against the gritty floor that smelled of pine, her toes lumps of ice in her cheesy sneakers and the underwire of her cheap bra jabbing into her side.

If they had to take her to the hospital, she thought dizzily, her underwear would be clean, but it would be frayed.

Whoa. No hospital thoughts, Annie ordered herself. Think macaroni and cheese. Peanut butter and jelly.

Mashed potatoes and gravy. Sometimes merely thinking of comfort food brought comfort.

The hand holding hers squeezed, and Annie turned her head to look into the eyes of the woman lying on the floor beside her. She didn't look harried anymore, not with her pale face and too-wide eyes. She looked afraid.

"I should have had Pop-Tarts instead of Special K this morning." Annie read the words on the woman's lips more than heard them, she was whispering that quietly.

Despite her still-churning stomach, Annie's mouth twitched in amusement. Apparently food had come to the other woman's mind, too. But more, she knew immediately what the woman meant. Suddenly, life was too precious to spend worrying about the circumference of your thighs.

Annie mouthed back to her. "No more store-brand ice milk for me. I'm gonna go for the good stuff."

From the front of the bank, another gunshot. More of the ceiling fell. "Hurry up!" the gunman shouted.

Annie glanced at her new friend. The other woman's pupils were even more dilated. Annie tightened her grip on the icy fingers. "Let's think about something else," she whispered. "I'm planning a shopping spree at a fancy lingerie store."

When the woman didn't seem to hear her, Annie tried again, thinking of her crummy tennies. "And shoes. I'm going to buy some nice shoes."

That caught her partner's interest. Her eyes focused. "Shoes," she breathed.

Annie squeezed her fingers again. "At full price."

The woman stared at Annie's face and held onto

her hand like it was a lifeline. "You're right," she said. "I have things to do."

And Annie knew what the other woman meant by that too. Not "things to do" in the sense of a list of chores or errands. But "things to do" in the sense of things to accomplish or experience.

"Yes," she whispered. "Think about what you have to do."

The other woman spoke again. "I didn't kiss my husband goodbye this morning and it's almost Valentine's Day." The anguish on her face twisted Annie's heart.

She hadn't kissed anyone goodbye that morning either. Annie didn't *have* anyone to kiss goodbye.

When her mother had retired, she'd moved from the cottage they'd shared to an apartment closer to town. Now Annie lived alone and a romantic life was something she realized she'd been waiting patiently for, too.

It seemed a shame—no, more than that—a *crime* to have been on the earth this long and never loved.

Sirens sounded in the distance. The gunman shouted again. His black shoes moved past Annie once more, this time in such a rush that the hem of his pants fluttered. A loud clank signalled he'd left the bank through the heavy front doors.

Someone started crying. A man muttered, "Thank God, thank God, thank God." The customers remained glued to the floor though, probably waiting for the police to arrive and tell them it was safe to move.

Annie shut her eyes, feeling her heart lurch as it restarted, feeling her blood begin moving through empty veins. Then emotion bubbled, bringing her even more alive, and whether it was relief or anger, or some potent combination of the two, the feeling made Annie surge to her feet. Her gaze snagged on a nearby hunk of fallen acoustical tile and then moved upward, to a yawning, jagged hole in the ceiling.

That's a *bullet* hole, she thought to herself. The man had a real gun that could really and truly have killed her. She might have died wearing discount clothing and dreaming of gourmet ice cream. And with regrets. Regrets that she'd never loved a man. Her stomach roiled again.

Annie extended her hand to help up her new friend, though the others around them remained waiting, still belly-down on the floor. Annie shook her head. She wasn't going to do any more waiting, not if she could help it. She had things to do and she was no longer going to postpone them.

Life was too darned short.

Griffin Chase, corporate attorney and vice-president of Chase Electronics, squeezed the receiver of the phone, its plastic edges biting hard into his palm. "*What?* She *what?*"

He'd left some papers at the family home this morning, forcing him to rush away from his office at Chase Electronics to retrieve them. With his parents and the housekeeping staff on vacation, he'd naturally picked up the ringing phone, only to find himself in a strange conversation with a detective from the Strawberry Bay Police Department.

Now the man patiently went through the facts all over again. Earlier that morning, an armed gunman had robbed the Savings and Loan branch at Kettering and Pine. The customers in the bank at the time—witnesses—were in transport to the police department to give their statements. And Annie Smith, little Annie Smith, the daughter of their former housekeeper, was one of those witnesses.

"She gave the officer in charge this number," Detective Morton said. "We're calling families to come in. It might reassure the witnesses to see a friendly face after their ordeal."

Ordeal. Griffin squeezed the phone again, remembering shy, quiet little Annie Smith. He wasn't even quite sure he knew how old she was now.

"I've been working out of the country for two years and just returned to town earlier this week," Griffin said, still trying to take it all in. "Did you say a robbery like this one has happened before?" Good God. Just a few months before, Strawberry Bay had been rattled by earthquakes. Now this.

The other man's voice turned professionally cautious. "I can't say for sure that it's the same robber, but the M.O. is the same. Anyway, sir—"

"I'll be there shortly." Griffin was already digging for his car keys.

"Or, since you're not related to her, Mr. Chase, I can have her call you if she truly needs assistance," the detective suggested.

That image of a slight, big-eyed Annie sprang into his head once more. "I'll be there shortly," he said again. Then he tossed the phone back onto its receiver, dashed down the stairs and headed for his car.

When a paddy wagon pulled up to the sprawling, one-story police complex, Griffin was already inside the building, propped against the lobby wall and staring through its smoked-glass windows. As an officer opened the back doors of the vehicle, Griffin pushed away from the wall and strolled toward the lobby entrance, his hands shoved in his pockets.

His eyes narrowed as people slowly descended from the vehicle. Would he recognize her? She had to be twenty-something now, because he remembered his mother saying she'd gone to cooking school and was running a catering business from the housekeeper's cottage on the estate.

But he hadn't caught a glimpse of her since returning a few days ago. Even though he was back home, the cooperative deals he'd brokered between Chase Electronics and several Pacific Rim countries during the past two years continued to consume his time and attention.

A young woman with wavy, blondish-brown hair and big brown eyes jumped from the paddy wagon. He glimpsed a small, triangular-shaped face and his belly clenched. Even as she turned to help someone else out, he was certain.

Annie. He recognized her—no, it was more than that. He *knew* her.

Without thinking, Griffin found himself pushing through the glass doors and hurrying down the cement steps. An officer held out a hand. "You'll have to stay away from the witnesses, sir."

Griffin didn't take his gaze off Annie. Yes, it had to be Annie. She wore slim-fitting black pants topped with a hip-length blouse that buttoned down the side and was printed with brightly colored kitchen utensils.

As she peered into the paddy wagon, she gave herself a hug as if she was cold.

"I'm her attorney," he said shortly, nodding in her direction.

At the sound of his words, she stilled. "Griffin?" She turned, and her silky brows rose over her pretty brown eyes.

He was surprised she had recognized his voice. Hers was throaty and soft, a woman's voice. He didn't associate it with the bashful little girl, clinging to her mother's hand, who had arrived at the estate all those years ago.

He saw her swallow and color rushed up her cheeks. "Wh-what are you doing here?" She swallowed again. "I don't need an attorney."

He moved forward and touched her shoulder. Though it strangely reassured him that beneath the starchy fabric of her blouse she felt solid and warm, he'd never noticed how delicate a woman's shoulder could be. Little Annie Smith's shoulder. "You gave the police the house number. They called."

"Oh." Her face flushed deeper. "I guess I said it automatically. My mother…"

"Worked there for eighteen years. It would be natural in a time of stress to rattle it off."

Lord. Little Annie Smith had actually been a witness to an armed bank robbery. Griffin's belly clenched again. He thought maybe she swayed a bit, so he wrapped his arm around her shoulders.

There. That probably made her feel better. Her blondish hair tickled his chin. "Let's get you inside."

Griffin had known Annie Smith since she was four years old and he was eleven. She'd come to live on his parents' estate when her mother became the family housekeeper. Though he'd never paid much attention to her, he remembered her following him around a time or two. She'd been much younger, and a girl, so he'd mostly ignored her.

But now a breath of a light, sweet scent and the sensation of her warm body against his arm and his side made it quite clear that Annie Smith wasn't a little girl anymore. Griffin frowned. He shouldn't be noticing something like that about Annie. She wasn't his type.

After two years out of the country, two years of virtually non-stop traveling and dealmaking to position the family company for even greater success in the next decade, he was glad to be home in California. There was still more work to be done—as always, he looked forward to it—but he planned to carve out a little time to play or he was going to be a very dull boy, indeed.

He'd already made a few get-reacquainted phone calls to the kind of women he did well with. Sophisticated women who knew what Griffin's commitment to the company meant he could offer—occasional opportunities for conversation, companionship and sex when the attraction warranted it. Sophisticated women who knew what he didn't offer—marriage.

So he had no business seeing Annie Smith—whose big, trusting Bambi eyes and soft mouth told him exactly what kind of hearth-and-husband woman she was—as a…well, *woman*. He inhaled another breath of that subtle, sweet scent of hers and almost groaned. It was vanilla. She smelled of sugar and vanilla. No wonder she made his mouth water.

But she's the hearth-and-husband type, he reminded himself. Don't forget that. For a man who worked intensely and had sex casually, it was better to think of her as that quiet, bashful kid.

They were steered toward the desk of the police officer who had phoned him. A woman in a no-nonsense business suit lingered nearby and introduced herself as Agent Blain of the FBI. But she gestured toward the man seated behind the desk. "The officer will be asking the questions, Ms. Smith. You tell Detective Morton everything you remember and then we'll get you out of here."

Annie seemed to remember her morning in clear detail. She'd catered the mayor's monthly staff breakfast, then headed for the Savings and Loan.

Griffin studied her face while she talked. If he'd been asked to describe her from memory, he would have said "average." Average height, average build, average blondish-brown hair of average length. A sweet-looking kid. She used to wear her hair in two pigtails tied with pink yarn.

He remembered the pink yarn and pigtails.

She didn't wear her hair like that anymore, though. Now the wavy, chin-length stuff was tucked behind her ears.

And Annie had cheekbones. High cheekbones that angled to a small chin that matched her small pert nose. Her mouth was small, too, but full and soft-looking and it was the color of that pink yarn he suddenly remembered so very well.

Griffin shifted restlessly against the vinyl seat of his chair. He shouldn't be looking at Annie's mouth. Most certainly not at a time like this.

To punctuate the thought, he suddenly picked up on her first hesitation in answering the questions about the robbery. Griffin straightened and paid more attention as the detective repeated himself. "Was there anything about the man you recognized, Annie?"

Her brow furrowed and her soft, pink mouth turned down. "I don't...think so." She frowned deeper. "Something..." Then she shook her head and her voice was more decisive. "No. I didn't recognize him. At first it was just that mask, and then I only saw his shoes. That's all I could see, really."

"Could you describe the shoes?" the detective asked.

"Black men's shoes that laced." She looked around the room, stuffed with desks and chairs and other officers interviewing other witnesses. "Like those." Her forefinger indicated a pair on a man one desk away, and then pointed again. "And those...and those."

She peered down at Griffin's cordovan loafers, then shrugged and looked back at the detective. "Sorry."

"That's all right, Annie. You did great." With a smile, Detective Morton reached across the desk and patted her hand.

Griffin frowned. Damn. The detective's smile was gleaming brighter than the shine of the fluorescent light off his bald spot.

Then Annie smiled back, and a dimple showed up, just at the left corner of her mouth. He'd never known Annie had a dimple. Or never noticed.

Frowning again, he leaned over and grabbed her wrist to tug her hand away from the detective's. Then

Griffin stood, pulling her up with him. "Can we go now?" he said abruptly.

Detective Morton rose to his feet, too, his gaze still on Annie. Griffin felt another spurt of annoyance. The other man was obviously sucking in his gut. It had to be unethical for a cop to hit on a witness, but despite that, it was more than professional interest written all over the detective's face.

"One last thing, Annie," Morton said.

Her eyebrows rose. "Yes?"

"I could put you in touch with a victim's support group," he said. "You might want to talk with other people about your experience. People trained to help you, and people who have gone through something similar."

Instead of answering the detective, Annie jerked her head toward Griffin.

"Sorry," he said hastily, suddenly aware he'd painfully tightened his grip on her wrist. Gritting his teeth, he forced his fingers to relax.

"Thank you," Annie said to the detective, flashing that dimple at him again. "But I'm going to be just fine. I *am* fine."

Now Griffin could breathe. Just for a second there, with the notion of Annie being a *victim,* he'd felt…a tad concerned.

But she'd said it herself. She was fine.

Which was why he didn't feel the need to talk much as they left the station beyond, "I'll give you a ride to your car." When they reached his Mercedes, however, he did open the passenger door and politely help her into the leather bucket seat.

Before he could shut the door, though, she touched his arm. "Would you mind putting the top down?"

He cocked an eyebrow. While February in coastal California was mild—the temperature was probably near seventy today—women usually liked the convertible's top up and the air-conditioning on, if necessary. The hair issue, he always figured.

But apparently Annie was different. "I want to feel the wind on my face," she said.

With a shrug, he complied with her request, and in a couple of minutes they were turning out of the police-station parking lot. The sun on their faces and the wind in their hair, they started down a fairly busy two-lane road.

Griffin sucked in a huge breath of fresh air and relaxed. Hell, but the sun felt good. With only one hand on the wheel, he rubbed his neck, trying to ease the tension slowly unknotting.

He slid a glance at Annie. Her head was against the back of the seat, her eyes were closed, and that pink mouth wore a little smile.

She'd said she was fine. She *looked* fine.

His muscles loosened even more. Now that she was safely in his car, he didn't mind admitting that he'd been somewhat bothered by the idea of little Annie Smith being the witness to a bank robbery. Then once he'd seen her again, seen how she'd grown up into a young woman who was still quiet and composed but also so pretty and so delicate, well, he'd downright hated the idea of Annie being shaken up.

"Hey, I'm glad you're okay," he said.

"Oh, I am."

Griffin glanced over at her again. She had her eyes

open now, and her cheeks were pink, from either the sun or the wind or both. In each of her hands she held one of the small white sneakers she'd been wearing.

Funny.

It wasn't so funny when she cocked back her arms and tossed them over the side of the car.

At first, Griffin's lips couldn't move, but his gaze darted to the rearview mirror to see the shoes tumbling along the side of the road behind them. Then his wits returned, and he shifted his foot to the brake pedal, abruptly slowing the car. "Annie—"

The vehicle behind them honked at their sudden change in speed, then pulled around to pass. "Annie—"

The vehicle behind that one honked, too, and the driver flipped Griffin an angry gesture as he passed them as well. With the shoes now several hundred feet behind and the traffic starting to pile up, Griffin gritted his teeth and moved his foot back to the accelerator. "Damn it, Annie," he said. "You threw your shoes out of the car."

"So sue me," she answered.

Griffin stared. Maybe the bank robber had kidnapped his nice, quiet Annie Smith—so composed and so delicate, he'd just thought—and put this suddenly flip woman in her stead. "That's littering," he felt compelled to point out. "It's illegal."

"I think Detective Morton would let me off, don't you?"

Griffin's eyebrows rose. That was all he had time for, because then Annie grabbed his arm and pointed toward the gourmet-ice-cream shop up ahead. "Stop there."

"Are you okay?" he asked.

"I told you, I'm fine." She squeezed his arm again. "But I want ice cream. Please. I want ice cream *now*."

There was no denying that the opposite sex had interested Griffin all his life. He'd first kissed a girl at eleven, he'd first dated at thirteen and women had only become more fascinating from there. Twenty years had passed since that novice kiss, and he'd been paying attention through every one of them. He knew not to mess around when a woman spoke in that decisive tone of voice.

He braked to a stop in front of the small shop with a wide front window that proclaimed in gilded letters Strawberry Bay's Supreme Ice Cream. Annie hopped out in her stocking feet. "Do you want something?" she asked.

He shook his head, baffled.

Her dimple winked at him as she unfastened a couple of buttons at her neck, and then she crossed her arms in front of her to grasp the hem of her long blouse. With a quick movement, she whipped the garment over her head and tossed it down on her seat, revealing the black V-neck T-shirt she wore beneath it. Then she twirled on her white socks and dashed into the shop.

All the speedy movement left Griffin's head spinning.

It couldn't be that Annie's neat little body made him dizzy. Certainly he'd noticed that women had breasts before. Lots of them had trim waists and hips. Still, it was disconcerting to find that sometime when he was away, or maybe before that, when he wasn't looking, Annie had developed the kind of pert, up-thrusting breasts and gently curving hips that were hard to look away from.

He ran a hand through his hair and forced his gaze off the door of the shop. What did it matter what Annie looked like? Annie was Annie. Annie the housekeeper's daughter. Little girl Annie.

Annie all grown-up.

He pushed that thought away, and it wasn't really so hard to think of her as a kid again when she was suddenly back in her seat, an enormous cone in her hand. "Double double chocolate fudge," she said, with all the relish of a child for a special treat.

When her tongue snaked out of her womanly mouth for a taste though, he hastily looked away and started the car. "No time for breakfast this morning?" he asked lightly.

She swallowed. "I wanted ice cream."

"Fine." Then he hesitated. She'd used that word too, she'd said she was "fine," but something about the shoes and the sudden urge for sweets made him just the slightest bit edgy again. "Are you sure you're all right, Annie?"

"Mm."

He pulled out of the parking lot and back onto the road. Her mumble sounded positive, but it didn't do much for his edgy mood. He wanted to be assured that her experience this morning hadn't affected her. Because, strangely enough, he had a terrible premonition that *that* might affect *him*.

Griffin cleared his throat. "Sure?"

"Mm." She made that same sound again.

He glanced over, and instantly figured out why she

wasn't giving him a straight answer. She was already pretty well occupied juggling that cone with one hand while the other snaked up the front of her T-shirt. When that hand quickly reappeared, she transferred the cone to it and then the now-free hand disappeared, worming its way into her short sleeve and then…down.

Griffin hoped like hell that the road remained clear before him, because he couldn't have looked away to save his life. He'd heard about this—among men it was almost a locker-room joke—but as he himself had never been witness to it before, he'd always considered it an urban—er, gender?—legend.

But now he knew it to be true. Because, after Annie took an emergency lick of her melting cone and after she executed one or two little shimmies, out the sleeve of her T-shirt came her hand, and in her hand was…her bra.

Which, of course, she immediately tossed over the side of the Mercedes.

As he watched in the rearview mirror the piece of white cotton depart, fluttering in the breeze, Griffin tried not to believe that his peace of mind wasn't getting away that easily, too.

Despite the warm sun, he felt the distinct beginnings of a chill. "Uh—" He had to clear his throat to get her name out. "Annie?"

"Are you okay?" she asked. "Is something the matter?"

She was stealing his lines. Worse, she was stealing his sense of well-being. "I'm just wondering about the, uh, this sudden need to divest yourself of, uh…"

She laughed, a delicious, free little giggle that

would have reassured him if he'd ever imagined that quiet Annie-Smith-the-housekeeper's-daughter could make such a sound. "Oh, Griffin," she said.

She patted his arm encouragingly. He caught sight of that unexpected little dimple again. He refused to let his gaze fall any lower than her mouth.

"I'm just tired of waiting," she said.

Waiting for what? That chill grew stronger, cold prickles gathering force at the nape of his neck.

Her honey-colored hair swirling around her cheeks, she threw her free arm in the air, wiggling her fingers in the wind. "From now on, my life is never going to be the same!"

With the power of a waterfall, the cold prickles poured down Griffin's back. Though he'd never before considered himself a superstitious man, he suddenly had the terrible feeling that *his* life would never be the same either.

Chapter Two

Annie pulled her face out of her pillow and opened one eye. Bright sunshine flooded her bedroom and she quickly squeezed the eye shut against the piercing light and moaned.

She was hungover, she thought, as that peek of daylight echoed painfully in her brain. Not from anything alcoholic, but from adrenaline, she supposed, or stress. She'd run on nerves gone wild yesterday, cleaning closets, counters, floors and then cooking until well past midnight. After that, she'd fallen into bed, too tired to even dream of the robbery.

The robbery.

Both eyes popped open and she breathed through another startling shock of sunlight. Yesterday she'd actually witnessed an armed man rob a bank.

As she pulled the bedcovers closer around her, the

event replayed in her mind, even to the churning of
her stomach and the sharp tang of pine cleaner in her
nose.

Think of something else, she commanded herself.
Anything other than the surprise and the fear. Think
of the ride in the paddy wagon. Even think of the
almost surreal experience of being questioned by the
police and the FBI.

The safe, protective police station. The nice detective behind the desk and Griffin Chase acting law-
yerly—no, acting like a sleek but threatening guard
dog, really—by her side.

Annie closed her eyes again and sank deeper into
the mattress, wishing it could swallow her up. Because, after the police had let her leave, what had she
done? Given poor Griffin a heart attack by tossing
items of clothing out of his car. She pulled the sheet
over her hot face.

She'd thrown her *bra,* for mercy's sake.

Wallowing in embarrassment, she recalled the uneasiness filling his blue eyes. The man hadn't seen
her in two years, and while to her he seemed as elegant and cool as always—his brown hair with its dark
gold streaks shorter than before, but his body's lean
strength and latent sense of power just the same—to
him she'd likely appeared at least dotty if not downright crazed.

What must he think of her?

Probably nothing, a little voice inside her answered
reasonably. In the past, he'd never noticed her, let
alone thought about her. Now, outside of thinking he
was obligated to do a favor for the daughter of a

family retainer, he probably didn't think anything about her either.

"Right," Annie said aloud, flipping the sheet back down and then kicking the covers entirely away. "Griffin's likely already put me and anything I did out of his mind."

Just as she was going to put the robbery out of her mind.

And Griffin.

Determined to get on with her day, she strode into her small bathroom. Its faint anti-bacterial smell testified to her housekeeping mania the day before, and it wasn't until she'd soaped, shampooed and toweled off that she comprehended just how far that mania had taken her.

She had cleaned out her underwear drawer yesterday, too. Working with the zeal of the newly converted, she'd ferreted out each ragged or ill-fitting bra, each pair of panties with sagging elastic or in a color so unappealing that they had overflowed the sale bins at the local discount store.

Which meant that Annie had thrown away all of it. Yes. Every stitch of undergarment she owned was now lying in her garbage can, in a ragged tangle of ugly colors and stretched-out straps.

And it wasn't as if she could rescue a piece of it for even a short shopping exhibition, Annie thought in dismay, wrapped in a towel and staring at the contents of her garbage. Because after the underwear drawer she'd moved on to cleaning out her freezer. That ragged tangle was now drenched with two cartons of melted neapolitan two-percent ice milk.

With nothing left to do but get something on and

get to the mall ASAP, Annie hurriedly dressed in a knee-length denim skirt and a dark blue T-shirt. There was no reason to imagine she couldn't make it to the store and back without detection or embarrassment, she told herself firmly. Hey, and the good news was she wouldn't have panty lines!

Still, she was slightly disconcerted by the weird sensation of air passing over her bare...uh...well, *there,* as she slung her purse over her shoulder and made a beeline for the door. She pulled it open, stepped out and—

Bumped into Griffin's chest.

"Good morning." His voice rumbled against the tip of her nose.

Annie leaped back, causing air to whirl up her skirt which in turn made her acutely conscious of all she wasn't wearing. "Uh, hi." She tried forgetting that delicious breath of his understated, expensive scent in her lungs as she pasted the insides of her knees together and threw a casual arm across her chest. "Um, I was just on my way out."

Oh, great, Annie, she thought, groaning inwardly. *Yesterday weird, today rude.*

He looked down at her, that same expression she'd labeled before as uneasiness again in his eyes. "So I didn't imagine it, did I? You really did grow up."

"H-huh?" Annie swallowed and pressed her forearm closer against her unbound breasts. "I mean, um, well, yes. I suppose I did."

She had been grown-up two years ago as well, but Griffin had looked right through her or over her or around her since the day she'd arrived at the Chase estate. Not in a superior, I'm-too-good-for-you way, but in a you're-a-little-girl-and-I-smell-a-potential-pest way.

She hadn't blamed him, though it hadn't stopped her from following him around, either.

He just hadn't noticed.

And while she remembered wanting him to notice her with an almost-humiliating intensity since she was four years old, today, in her underwearless state, she wished she could simply disappear before his eyes.

But he *was* noticing something, darn it, as he slowly shook his head. "When did you stop wearing..."

How could he tell? Annie's heart froze and she squeezed her knees even more tightly together as she watched his forefingers make puzzling circles beside his ears.

"...pigtails you call them, right?" He smiled.

Oh my. She'd forgotten Griffin's smile. It tilted up one corner of his mouth and both corners of his blue, blue eyes. Over the years she'd seen him smile that smile a hundred times—at her mother when finagling more cookies, at one of the groundsmen for washing and waxing his car, at every girl he'd ever brought home.

He'd just never smiled that smile at her. Not the housekeeper's daughter.

"Annie?"

"Wow," Annie murmured, then caught herself, blinking away her smile-induced stupor. "Oh. Yes. What?"

"Annie?" he said again, probably wondering if there was a padded room nearby. "Are you all right?"

She desperately cast back to the conversation. Pig-tails. "Pigtails. You're exactly right. That's what they're called." She lifted both hands to imitate those funny ear circles he'd made.

And then remembered her bralessness and immediately clapped both arms across her chest, as if she was hugging herself.

Griffin's expression switched from doubt to concern. "Are you cold? Why don't we go inside?"

We? *We?* But even with that warning, Annie did nothing as he stepped closer except step back, until they were both inside the small front room of her cottage and he'd shut the door behind him.

Now what was she supposed to do with him? It didn't seem quite fitting for the wealthy man-about-town to be standing in her modest cottage.

"Well, um, would you like to sit down?" she felt forced to ask.

"Sure." He dropped onto the flowered cushions of her white wicker love seat, settling against its back and extending his long legs.

Oh, terrific. Not only did his position not make him seem any less out-of-place, it made it clear that he planned to stay awhile. She bit her bottom lip. "And some coffee? Would you like some coffee?" If he was going to stick around even for a few minutes she needed some alone time in her comforting kitchen to catch her breath and find her composure.

"Sure," he said again.

Though trying to keep her legs together made her walk a sort of awkward scurry, Annie hurried off, wondering if she could stitch temporary undergarments from paper towels and the cook's twine she used for her famous parmesan chicken rollups. She was biting her lip and contemplating the paper towels when Griffin suddenly appeared in the kitchen.

"Can I help?" he asked.

The largest room of the cottage suddenly shrank and Annie spun toward her coffeemaker. "Oh, no. This will just take a minute."

He didn't get the hint, instead pulling up one of her kitchen stools to the countertop nearby. "So you became a cook?"

She sneaked a peek at him, for the first time absorbing the fact that he was wearing a comfortable-looking, almost baggy pair of khakis and a white T-shirt that had the luxurious sheen of silk. The soft leather slip-ons on his feet probably cost more than all the shoes in her closet put together.

"Well, I'd like to think I've been a cook for a long time," she answered, sounding less nervous than she felt. "I *became* a caterer, thanks to your parents. When the new housekeeper didn't want to live on the estate, they rented me the cottage at a rate that made starting my own business possible."

Whew. It was much easier talking to him when she could half turn away and keep busy with the coffee. "How about you?" she asked. "Anything new about you in the last two years?"

Good. The question sounded automatic and impersonal. No way could Griffin guess that she'd trolled for every factoid she could get from his parents and his brother during the last twenty-four months. Old habits died hard, she'd rationalized then.

But now she blew all her fake disinterest by adding,

"I thought you weren't supposed to be back until June tenth."

He didn't seem to detect her slip. "Believe me, I'm more than happy that I made it back to California early."

Annie sprinkled some cinnamon over the freshly ground coffee beans and swung the filter basket into place then pressed the button marked Brew. "Why? Were you that ready to come home?" She suppressed a little teen-ish rush of delight that he hadn't found some exotic lover impossible to leave behind.

"That too, I suppose, and I was gratified to wrap up my business deals early. But who would have come to your rescue yesterday if I hadn't been back?"

Annie felt her face heat. "I should have thanked you for that right away, though I didn't really need *rescuing*."

"Oh, I don't know. If you'd added flagging down a ride to eating ice cream and divesting yourself of clothing, I can imagine all sorts of emergencies that might have come up." There was a hint of amusement in his voice.

Okay, so maybe her actions deserved Griffin's teasing—something she would have lopped off her right ear for when she was seventeen—but she was really starting to regret yesterday's vows. It was one thing for a woman to kick off her shoes and splurge on double double chocolate fudge. It was entirely another to be left braless and pantyless while having a conversation about disrobing with the one man said woman had mooned over for almost her entire life.

"I shouldn't razz you though, Annie," Griffin continued. "To be honest, I'm mad as hell that you had to go through that experience at all."

Annie concentrated on sliding away the coffee carafe so that the dark, fragrant stream of liquid flowed into a thick mug instead. "I'm trying not to think of it too much myself." An image of the gun flashed in her mind, and she suppressed a shiver while coffee trickled into a second mug.

With two mugs full and the carafe replaced, Annie finally had to face Griffin. Carrying a mug in each hand, she walked the few steps toward him, watching that she didn't spill instead of watching him. She put one coffee against the countertop and slid it his way. "Maybe I'll just pretend yesterday didn't happen."

"I don't think that will work, Annie," Griffin said softly.

She looked up, meeting his gaze. "No?"

"*I* can't forget."

Mercy. She'd never been this close to him, and with only two feet of countertop between them, his eyes mesmerized her. Their blue was faceted with clear crystal, and his eyelashes, like his hair, were edged in gold. "You can't forget what?" she said, trying to break the spell.

"You said you were tired of waiting."

"Oh."

"I just can't help wondering what for."

"Oh," she said again. "Well…" She'd been tired of waiting for shoe sales. Tired of waiting for the someday when she deserved nice lingerie. But most of all, she'd been tired of waiting for love to enter her life. For a man. "That kind of talk was just a reaction. That's all. I think."

"You think?"

Annie squeezed her mug of coffee between her palms. In the light of a new day, didn't it seem more sensible—safer—to return to old, familiar paths? She shrugged. "I'm sure. And I'm over the robbery already."

His eyebrows rose. "Then I suppose you won't mind seeing this." He watched her carefully, though, as he pulled something from his back pocket. A newspaper, creased three times, that he unfolded and then put in her free hand.

The *Strawberry Bay Bulletin.* Annie dropped her gaze to the front-page photo and then dropped her mug, not even hearing it crash and break into fragments against the tile floor. Instead, as she looked at the photo of the bank lobby with the massive, jagged holes in its ceiling, Annie was hearing the sound of the robbery. It was the sound of the gunfire and the well of terrified silence and that voice almost sobbing "Thank God, thank God, thank God," all rolled into one ball of nearly unbearable noise.

She closed her eyes and put her hands over her ears and then suddenly someone was holding her. Griffin. He was warm and he was big and she couldn't believe she was gluing herself against him, but there it was.

It was his luxurious, sandalwood-and-something-else scent that finally dispelled the remembered stench of gunfire and it was his voice, "I'm sorry, Annie. So sorry, Annie," that finally banished the echoes of yesterday's sounds.

His big hand was rubbing her back and she finally found the nerve to look up at him. She tried a smile, but it quickly wobbled off. "I guess I'm not as over it as I thought."

"I shouldn't have sprung the picture on you like that." His hand smoothed down her back again.

She should move away, but her legs wouldn't seem to obey her mind's commands. And her mind! It wasn't behaving either. It seemed to have forgotten this was *Griffin Chase,* vice-president of Chase Electronics, the biggest employer in town, who she was snuggled up against. It seemed to have forgotten this was Griffin Chase, the unattainable prince in every one of her adolescent Cinderella dreams.

Instead, it registered heat and size and *male* and something inside her—something warm and liquid— seemed to be rising and falling all at once.

"Forgive me?" he asked. That one side of his mouth kicked up when he smiled, a bit rueful, and he started to run his hand a third time down her back.

A hand that abruptly halted midway. Midway, where a bra strap would usually be.

They both froze. Annie was suddenly, acutely aware not only of the lack of a bra strap, but also that her bare breasts were against his hard chest, with only two thin layers between them. At the thought, her nipples, nestled so closely to Griffin, tightened.

Oh, mercy. She jumped away from him, the soles of her shoes crunching against pieces of ceramic mug. Her face felt flushed and she crossed her arms over herself as she looked down at the mess on the floor. "I…" She couldn't think of anything to say.

"It's okay," he said. Maybe his voice was a bit hoarse, maybe not. "Let me take care of it."

Take care of what? But Annie's brain wasn't firing

with all the necessary cylinders even as he strode to the broom propped in one corner of the room and then strode back to start sweeping up the mess at her feet. She didn't prevent him from cleaning, but merely stepped clear of the debris as she giddily recalled the hardness of his chest and the heavy warmth of his hand and how comforting and…and…um, *pleasing* it had been to feel Griffin against her.

She didn't stop him from opening the cabinet under the sink, either. He had to toss the contents of the dustpan, after all, into the oversized white garbage pail.

The garbage pail that, she belatedly remembered, was almost overflowing with ice-cream-covered undergarments.

"Oh!" Annie said, dashing forward. She'd even gingerly pawed through the mess with tongs at one point, desperate for something wearable, so that several bras hung drunkenly over the edge to reveal a pile of ice-milk-sodden, but clearly recognizable panties. "I don't…I'm not…"

Griffin looked at her, his brows raised. "You don't?" He looked back at the contents of the can. "You're not?" He looked at her again. "I can…see that. I just don't understand why."

Why? How could she possibly tell him about what had gone through her mind yesterday when she was lying on the bank's floor? Annie chewed on her lower lip, feeling completely foolish about those silly vows. Then someone, a sainted someone in her book, rapped impatiently on her front door. Without a second's hesitation, Annie grabbed at the opportunity to escape what now seemed horribly embarrassing and completely unexplainable.

"Company!" she said brightly, pasting on a cheery smile. Then she turned and ran to see who it was, as if the man she'd once adored from afar hadn't just discovered her naughty, though totally innocent, secret.

On the other side of Annie's front door stood two dear, familiar figures—her mother, Natalie Smith, and Annie's best friend, Elena O'Brien. "Mom, Elena. Come in, come in."

With a surge of relief, Annie ushered them inside. They were just the people to remind her of the real Annie Smith. The ordinarily patient and ordinarily shy Annie Smith. She wasn't the unfamiliar creature who had tossed her clothes away yesterday any more than she was the half-naked woman who'd found herself in the arms of Griffin Chase this morning.

Her mother and Elena would help her remember that.

Annie's mom looked at Annie closely, an unfamiliar frown on her pretty face. "Honey? Are you all right? You look...different."

"No, I don't," Annie denied quickly. *I'm the same. Nothing has changed.* "I told you yesterday, Mom, I'm fine. A-okay. Peachy-keen. Hunky-dory."

"You left out tutti-frutti." Elena grinned, her sassy smile bright against the golden color of her skin. Her Mexican mother and Irish father accounted for her straight black hair and blue eyes.

"Still," Elena continued, "your mom wasn't going to stop worrying until I drove her over here. I told her nothing could shake you—" Her eyes widened as she caught sight of something over Annie's shoulder. "Whoa. Maybe I was wrong."

Annie swung around slowly to find Griffin coming into the room. It's not that she'd forgotten him, exactly, but she hadn't quite yet figured out how to explain his presence or how to respond to him. Particularly now that she knew he knew that what she wore beneath her skirt and T-shirt was exactly zippo.

But he took the uncomfortable situation out of her hands by walking directly to Annie's mom and lifting her off her feet in a grizzly-worthy bear hug.

"Griffin!" her mom cried. When he set her down she lifted up on her tiptoes to plant a kiss on his cheek. "You're home."

"And completely devastated to discover that in the two years I was gone you had retired." He smiled down at her. "Any chance I could entice you back? At least just to fill the cookie jar?"

Her mother laughed, and under the cover of their continuing conversation, Elena sidled over to Annie. "Is there something you want to tell me?"

Annie rolled her eyes. "I told you yesterday. He gave me a ride from the police station."

Elena's brows rose. "What about last night? Any additional, uh...rides?"

Annie lightly slapped her friend's arm. As if a man like him would look at her twice in that way! "Of course not. Griffin merely came over to check on me this morning. It was a neighborly thing to do."

Elena's eyebrows rose even higher. "Neighborly?" she asked, her voice skeptical.

Before she could scold her friend again, Griffin turned away from Annie's mom to look at the two younger women. "And this is?" He was asking for an introduction to Elena, but his gaze was only for Annie.

Suddenly, beneath her clothes, her skin prickled. She was naked. He knew it, she knew it, it was a secret only the two of them shared, and it only made her feel that much more exposed.

Annie swallowed as more tickles of awareness rose on her bare flesh. "Griffin, this is—this is my friend Elena O'Brien." She hoped her voice didn't sound as squeaky to them as it did to herself. "Elena, may I introduce you to Griffin Chase."

There was a funny little smile on Elena's face as she stuck out her hand to shake Griffin's. "Brother of Logan, I presume?"

That caught Griffin's attention. His eyes narrowed. "You know my little brother?"

Elena gave a casual wave of her fingers. "We go *way* back. Be sure to give him my best."

Annie slid a look at Elena. There was bad blood between Elena and Griffin's "little" brother—now twenty-nine years old and as big as Griffin himself— over a senior prom date gone awry, though Elena wouldn't speak of it beyond making nasty cracks about Logan whenever they happened to catch a glimpse of him.

Griffin glanced at Annie, then back at Elena. "Your best? I'll be sure to do that."

Annie's friend smiled once more but it wasn't her usual cheerful one. "Thank you. Be sure to tell him Elena says hello. That's Elena with an 'e' as in every day I thank my lucky stars he left me standing there."

Nodding, Griffin gave her one more half-puzzled,

half-amused look, then switched his attention to Annie. "I'll be on my way now," he said. "I brought piles of work home. Will you be okay?"

Those crystal-faceted blue eyes of his made it impossible for her to look away, and even more impossible to forget the sensation of being enclosed by his arms. "I wish people would stop asking me that," she whispered. It didn't seem necessary to talk any louder, not when she could have sworn there were only the two of them in the room, maybe in the whole world.

He shrugged, then his hand lifted and he brushed his fingertips across her temple to tuck a strand of hair behind her ear. His fingers were cool and his touch gentle. Goose bumps skittered across Annie's neck and then southward, and she found herself once again crossing her arms over her chest.

His gaze flicked down toward her breasts, back up to her eyes. "We're just concerned," he said softly. "You've been through a stressful experience."

"My mom and Elena are here." Somewhere. She remembered how relieved she'd been to see them, because they would remind her of the real, the patient, the so-very-ordinary Annie Smith. The Annie Smith who Griffin Chase had never looked at twice, though she'd followed him around since she was four years old. "So you see, I don't need a keeper or a…a…brother."

He blinked. "A brother."

Annie felt herself flushing. "Or whatever."

Griffin smiled, and Annie thought he suddenly appeared more relaxed.

"You're right," he said. "I'm certain you don't

need a keeper, or a brother, or a 'whatever.'" Cool fingertips brushed her temple again. "Goodbye Annie."

Then he was gone.

With the click of the door behind him, her mother and Elena started chattering, as if to fill up the hole his leaving created. Their talk went on around her: Annie's impending twenty-fifth birthday and how to celebrate it; her big catering job for the elder Chases' fortieth wedding anniversary; the most recent phone call Annie's aunt had made to Annie's mom. Instead of joining in, Annie wandered to the window.

Over the lace café curtains, she could see Griffin stride away. As she watched, she thought of his crystal-blue eyes and how they made her skin tingle and how that tingle made her feel alive and even… yes…*impatient*. Then he disappeared into the thick stand of oaks that separated her cottage from the Chase's house.

There was a drive that connected the two residences as well, but the shortest foot route was the way he'd chosen, through the oaks. It would take him past a trellised gazebo, then up the steps to the veranda that encircled the big house.

Formally named the Montgomery Mansion, the Chase's massive three-story Victorian with its leaded windows and gingerbread fretwork was listed on the national historic register. In modern times, an adjacent carriage house had been replaced by a fleet-worthy garage embellished with similar Victorian styling. The old carriage house had been moved to the other side of the oaks then renovated as the housekeeper's residence. It was Annie's now.

Griffin, master-of-the-manor Griffin, lived in the mansion while Annie, silly, tingling Annie lived in the cottage. A distance not easily breached, but she'd been watching through windows across it all her life.

She whirled away from the window and tuned in to her mother and Elena.

"...my sister keeps insisting I should move to San Diego and share her condominium. It's right on the beach. Some place called the Silver Strand."

Elena flopped onto the love seat, her straight black hair flying up then settling back into place against her jaw. "The Silver Strand. It sounds heavenly. Why don't you take her up on it, Natalie?"

Annie's mom laughed. "Oh, I couldn't. I'm staying in Strawberry Bay."

Annie studied her mother. Though she'd retired when the arthritis in her hands made her housekeeping duties difficult, she remained slim and pretty. She didn't look much older than the woman whose husband had walked out on her so long ago. Yet Natalie Smith had never dated another man or even appeared interested in one.

What was her mother waiting for? Annie mused.

Waiting. That was Annie, too, of course, and she might as well be preparing to celebrate her seventy-fifth birthday instead of her twenty-fifth for all the living she'd done. That truth had bothered her yesterday. She'd vowed to find love instead of waiting for it.

But her common sense had reasserted itself this morning. Yes, common sense...or cold feet?

Through the open window a breeze blew in and the air swept up Annie's skirt. The goose bumps rising on her bare flesh caused her to remember the tingles that Griffin's touch made burst across her skin.

Certainly he couldn't be the right man for her. He was merely the one she'd spun fantasies about, the prince a lonely little girl had put on a pedestal. But wouldn't it be wonderful to find another who made her feel that way? The breeze brushed by her again. Yet what if waiting patiently meant waiting forever?

"Elena," she said urgently.

Her mouth open in mid-sentence, Elena's head swiveled toward Annie. "Huh?"

"Come shopping with me." Though Elena was the sole support of her teenage sister and worked two jobs, she always managed to look chic.

Elena blinked. "Huh? What?"

Annie headed for her purse. "I need your help. New clothes. From the inside out. And from the department store, not the discount store."

She didn't miss the gleam in Elena's eyes. "It's a miracle!"

No, said a little voice inside Annie. *It's a man.*

She didn't know who quite yet, but she wanted one.

Despite her cowardly attempt at denial this morning, after yesterday's experience she was certain she wanted love. And she was no longer content to wait for it to find her.

Chapter Three

"Goodbye, Mother. Tell Dad I'll be waiting for his call in my office tomorrow." Shaking his head, Griffin hung up the phone, wondering if his mother would get the chance to pass along the message.

Though Laura and Jonathon Chase were vacationing in Hawaii, the way they spent their days seemed just as separate as when they were in California. He'd seen it with his own eyes on his way home from his stay abroad. He'd spent a few days at their house on the Big Island where he'd observed his father dedicating long hours to the golf course in the same intense manner he dedicated himself as CEO of Chase Electronics when he was in Strawberry Bay.

Griffin didn't know what his mother usually did with those hours alone in paradise, but today she was worrying about Annie. Did she seem bothered by the bank robbery? Did Griffin think she would be recovered enough to cater their upcoming fortieth anniversary party?

Griffin had nobly bitten back a question of his own. Why the hell his mother wanted to celebrate forty years of glacial matrimony was beyond him. Instead, he'd merely assured her that Annie appeared perfectly able to fulfill her obligations.

Now he just had to ensure that he didn't take another trek to her cottage to verify that assertion for himself.

Because he already knew she was fine. Naked, but fine.

No. Of course she wasn't naked. She'd been wearing clothes. Just nothing underneath them. And why that was and why it would so strongly capture his imagination was something better left alone.

With that resolve, Griffin opened a drawer and pulled out his address book. He would find something to do and someone—a woman—to do it with. After working at home all day yesterday and then spending a few hours in the office this morning, he should enjoy Sunday afternoon, after all. But then his gaze snagged on the calendar.

Not just any Sunday, damn it. It was the fourteenth. *February* fourteenth. A totally lethal day for any entrenched-for-eternity bachelor like himself. Taking a woman out on Valentine's Day was a statement, easily misread as a commitment for at least the rest of the year. He shuddered, quickly slapping shut his address book. If he wanted to reclaim his single-man, casual-with-women lifestyle—that his workaholic

ways suited him for—he couldn't take the risk of a
Valentine's Day date.

Which is why he was aimlessly wandering around
downstairs and considering heading back to the office
when his younger brother bounded through the front
door. "Hey, bro," Logan said. "Have you seen my
tennis racket?"

Griffin shoved his hands in the pockets of his
slacks, slid them out. He looked over his shoulder,
picked up his feet, then finally pulled at the front of
his shirt to peer down at his navel. "No. I haven't
seen your tennis racket."

"Ha. Ha. Very funny." Logan said. He jogged toward the staircase that led to his old room. "I can't
remember if I moved it to the condo or left it here."

Just bored enough to exert the energy it took to
follow, Griffin started climbing the first flight of stairs
after him. "Tennis with Cynthia, I presume?"

Logan froze on the landing, then looked back down
at Griffin, a horrified expression on his face. "That's
not funny either. This is Valentine's Day, have you
forgotten?"

"Well, uh, no." But Cynthia had been his brother's
girlfriend for ten years. From what his mother hinted
at, an engagement was just a nudge or two away.
"You're doing something with her later?"

Logan blinked, then spoke slowly, as if Griffin had
lost some brain cells. "Val…en…tine's…Day."

"I *know.*"

"Well then you know that Valentine's Day is lethal
to any firmly entrenched bachelor. You told me that
years ago. It's not something I've forgotten, Griffin."

Griffin felt a spurt of guilt. Was it right for him to have passed along to Logan his own romantic pessimism? "I know, Logan, but—"

"Gotcha." His brother grinned. "The truth is Cynthia herself declined to celebrate with me today. She's up for some local commercial tomorrow and she wants to spend all day in a cucumber—or was it carrot?—mask. But we did exchange appropriately mushy e-mails this morning."

Mushy e-mails? Griffin decided not to touch that with a ten-foot pole. "So who are you playing tennis with, then?"

"Tom Sullivan," Logan said. "He's the cop who talked Dad into sponsoring the mentor program at the company."

As their father's right hand, it was actually Logan who had convinced the old man to employ at-risk, though high-achieving, high-school students as interns at Chase Electronics. Some of those former students were already out of college and very successful in their own careers, thanks to the partnership between Chase Electronics and the Strawberry Bay Police Department.

Thinking of the police led Griffin naturally back to recent events. "Would your buddy Tom know anything about the investigation into the bank robbery?" Griffin had told Logan about it himself, when he'd finally returned to the office on Friday.

Logan shrugged. "I can ask. How's Annie doing, by the way?"

Griffin frowned. "How the hell should I know?" he asked in irritation, even though he'd wondered the same thing himself all morning, causing the report he'd been drafting to take twice as long.

Logan's eyebrows rose. "Hey, it was just a question." He glanced at his watch. "If I can find that racket, maybe I have time to check on—"

"Don't bother." For some reason, Griffin didn't want his Valentine's Day-free and not-completely-taken brother to visit Annie. "I'm going by there myself soon."

Thinking back on it, he remembered Logan tolerating Annie pretty well when they were kids. So Griffin didn't think it was fair for his brother to make a February fourteenth visit. She just might get the wrong idea.

"Whatever you say, pal." Logan gave him one strange, thoughtful look, then headed up the stairs.

Griffin headed down them. He'd told Logan that he'd check on Annie.

At least it was something to do.

It took just a few minutes to cut through the oaks and climb up Annie's steps. When he raised his hand to knock, the sound of loud, yet mild cursing floated through the closed front door. "Darn and darn and shoot, shoot, shoot!" Something clattered against the floor.

Eyebrows drawing together, Griffin knocked.

There was a moment of silence—an almost embarrassed silence, he imagined—and then the noise of odd, uneven footsteps. *Clop click clop click clop click.* Annie opened the door.

Griffin shoved his hands in his pockets, struck by an unbidden, unwelcome need to touch.

Honey-haired Annie was wearing pink. A soft, tal-cum-powder pink. A long-sleeved top criss-crossed her breasts and tied at the side of her waist like some-thing a ballet dancer would wear. It revealed a V of pale skin at her neck and a very modest swell of cleavage. The top was tight enough for Griffin to make out the thin outline of her bra.

Yesterday vividly came back to him. The pang in his chest when she'd broken down, the fragile warmth of her in his arms, his hand stroking her back and the sudden realization that his palm didn't bump over a bra strap. And then her realization of his realization. Her nipples had tightened into hard little pearls that had branded his skin.

Just the memory shot twin arrows of heat from his chest to his groin. Griffin set his jaw and ignored the sensation.

Forget all that. Think about today. She's wearing underclothes today.

But the discovery didn't make her any less ap-pealing, not when she was in a matching short, swingy skirt that revealed a length of slender legs. The *clop click clop* sound of her footsteps was ex-plained by the fact that the strap of one cute, high-heeled shoe was buckled, while the strap of the other shoe hung free.

He smiled at her, he couldn't help himself. "Happy Valentine's Day," he said, before thinking better of it.

Her cheeks flushed, pinker than her outfit. "Well, thanks. Same to you."

"I'm just checking in."

"Oh," she said, making a little face.

Another memory of the day before surfaced. Her big brown eyes wide, Annie had told him she didn't need a keeper or a brother or a "whatever."

Because she had a boyfriend?

He was annoyed that the thought hadn't occurred to him before. Just because there hadn't been a man in her cottage yesterday morning didn't mean she didn't have a man in her life. And Annie struck him as the type of woman who would be very particular about her bed partners, so if there was a man in her life, he wouldn't be a casual kind of man.

And she was all dressed up—in pink even—for Valentine's Day.

He tried peering over her shoulder to see evidence of standard February fourteenth fare, like flowers or candy. "Having a good day?"

She made that funny little face again. "Okay, I guess. I'm having trouble with my new shoe."

"Can I help?" Without waiting for an answer or an invitation, he moved forward. Inside the cottage he would be able to observe more boyfriend evidence. Maybe even be there when the guy came to pick her up. As her post-robbery rescuer it was certainly natural, almost imperative even, that he perform a thorough inspection of the man, Griffin decided.

"Okay." Blinking rapidly, Annie moved back, *click clop click*.

Shutting her door behind him, Griffin looked around. It appeared much the same as the day before. No flowers. No boxes of candy, no striped boxes from lingerie stores. Only Annie herself, looking like a perfectly sweet, perfectly tempting Valentine in all that pink.

And one imperfect shoe. She took it off and held it up. "I can't get the strap through the buckle."

With all the confidence of a man faced with a simple problem, he took the light piece of leather in his hand and made his way to the love seat. "I'm sure I can fix this in no time flat."

Hah. The delicate shoe with its even more delicate strap made him feel like each hand was the size and shape of a baseball mitt.

"I need a tool," he finally said, frowning at the stubborn strap. As slender as the damn thing was, he just couldn't feed it through the gold-toned buckle either. But with a tool a man was never at a loss.

"What kind of tool?"

He looked up. Annie had a tiny, concerned crease between her light-brown brows that he wanted to erase with the pad of his thumb. He wanted to touch her there, or that place on her cheek where a dimple would wink if she smiled, or at that very smooth, very sweet spot on her temple where he'd touched her yesterday, where he could see her pulse beating today.

Her mouth moved. He thought of touching her there, too. His thumb against that puffy surface, his forefinger painting the deep dip of her upper lip, his own mouth lowering—

Her lips moved again, and he heard the words she said this time. "What tool?" she prompted.

Griffin shook himself. God. Valentine's Day must be messing with his head. "Needle-nose pliers?"

She nodded and left the room, giving Griffin time

to take a few deep, get-his-brain-back-in-the-right-hemisphere breaths. When she returned with the requested tool, he focused purely on the problem at hand and had the strap threaded through the buckle in moments.

Without taking his gaze off the shoe, he set it on the floor. "Slip your foot in and I'll buckle it for you, then pull the strap through the other side."

After a hesitation, she obeyed. Encased in a sheer stocking and with each toenail painted a matching talcum pink, the foot slowly lifted. As she pointed it through the wide circle made by the strap, her standing leg wobbled. Griffin quickly knelt on the floor and she placed her hand on his shoulder for balance.

He went to work on fastening the shoe, his hands back to baseball mitts. Crouched next to her, he felt the warmth of her sleek leg against his cheek and the scent of her filled his lungs. It was cinnamon, he thought. Spicy yet still sweet. He felt a tremor run through her, but he wasn't sure if she was off-balance again or if his nearness affected her the way her nearness affected him.

Little Annie Smith, he reminded himself again.

Annie Smith all grown up, that evil little voice inside him answered.

He cleared his throat and used all his powers of concentration to ignore Annie in order to pull the strap through the second half of the buckle with the help of the needle-nose pliers. "Whew."

He dropped the tool on the floor and straightened just enough to take a seat on the cushions of her love seat. "Mission accomplished."

Annie didn't lift her eyes off the newly fastened shoe. He thought perhaps she was breathing a little fast, but since his breaths were coming even faster, he couldn't be sure. "Is it okay?" he forced himself to ask.

God forbid the shoe was too loose or too tight and she sent him to work on it once more. If he got that close to her legs again, he couldn't promise he wouldn't run his tongue along the pretty curve of her calf.

"I'm just wondering..." Annie started.

"Wondering?"

"If I'm going to have to wear this shoe to bed tonight."

To bed. A woman with a boyfriend would count on him to get it off her, wouldn't she? "You don't have a man to take care of that for you?"

Her head came up, and her brown eyes widened. "Oh! Oh, no." She blushed. "Well, maybe. But...not yet."

Griffin frowned. "What's that supposed to mean?"

Her blush deepened. "I'm kind of...shy. A watcher. So I usually hate Valentine's Day," she confessed.

He smiled. "We're soulmates then." It was on a Valentine's Day that he'd finally accepted the lesson of his parents' marriage. It was the day he'd finally accepted his own true nature.

Annie shook her head. "Somehow I doubt that, Griffin. But I'm determined to get over how I feel about the day." Her shoulders squared. "Did you know I'm almost twenty-five years old?"

Jail bait would be safer for him, but he'd figured she was somewhere in that range. "Congratulations."

"No congratulations are in order. That's the problem." She frowned, her soft, pink mouth pouting a little. "I've been waiting, you see. But today, *tonight,* I'm *seeking.*"

A small rush of alarm ran through him. "Seeking?"

"As a matter of fact, I'm beginning to think that the fact it's Valentine's Day is a good omen."

Valentine's Day and good omens didn't go together in his book, but he just said, "Exactly what are you doing tonight?"

"I'm going to a party." Her voice held a note of pride. "I, Annie Smith, on Valentine's Day, am going to a party as a seeker of…of love."

Griffin stared at her. A seeker of love? The idea struck him as horrifying. *Annie Smith seeking love.* Terrifying. Heading out on a day like today, full of romantic hope, could spell disaster for her. Who knew what kind of men were out there, ready to take advantage of such optimism?

"Do you have a date to escort you during this, uh, seeking?" he asked hoarsely.

She shook her head and then her chin came up a notch. "I'm going alone."

Griffin closed his eyes. "Oh no, you're not." Maybe this was payback for all those times he'd ignored her when she was a little girl. He vaguely remembered she'd lost her doll once and he'd refused to help her look for it. Whatever the reason, he couldn't send her out in the world alone.

Seeking.

God.

On *Valentine's Day*. She could get hurt.

Griffin sighed, stood up. ''Somebody's gotta be around to unbuckle your shoe.''

Annie had sputtered some half-hearted protests, but Griffin guessed that she was really grateful she didn't have to walk into the Valentine's Day party alone. Not long after he'd fastened her shoe, they found themselves outside the home of their hosts, a recently married couple who were friends of Annie's.

There was some sort of holdup at the door, and they stood behind a line of six or eight others who appeared equally puzzled by the delay. Annie introduced him to the couple in front of them and he was pleased to discover they weren't complete strangers. The male half was the brother of an old friend, while the man's date was the daughter of a golfing buddy of Griffin's father.

He'd forgotten how small Strawberry Bay really was. By tomorrow noon, it would be all over town that Griffin had escorted Annie to the party. If he wasn't careful, by tomorrow evening the gossips would concoct some sort of grand romance for the two of them.

Griffin subtly shifted farther away from her and put on his best big-brother expression. Maybe it was too late to question the wisdom of appointing himself her Valentine's Day protector, but he could make it clear to the partygoers that there was nothing the least bit passionate between them.

Then after tonight, he'd let her go.

As they shuffled closer to the front door, a round of infectious laughter had both Griffin and Annie shrugging and exchanging puzzled smiles. Not until they were at the front of the line did they understand what the giggles were all about.

Annie introduced Griffin to their smiling host, Jeff, and then the man explained what was happening. "It's a party game," he said, gesturing at the video camera set up on a tripod in the entry. "Everyone who attends as a couple is kissing on tape. We'll play the whole thing later and award prizes."

Jeff wiggled his eyebrows and his grin widened. "You know, best, worst, coldest, hottest."

Uh-oh, Griffin thought. He looked over at Annie.

She wasn't looking at him. "We don't want to play," she said quickly. Still without meeting his eyes, she took hold of Griffin's forearm and tried tugging him through the entry.

Jeff blocked their way, his good-natured grin still in place. "C'mon Annie. Be a good sport. It's not fun unless everybody plays."

She frowned, shaking her head.

But Jeff wouldn't give up. He elbowed Griffin in the ribs. "Griffin. You tell her. You gotta play. And you wanta play, right?"

Oh, hell. What was a man supposed to say? He knew Annie wasn't keen on kissing him for the camera. But they were holding up the line behind them by refusing and people were gathering closer to see what was happening. So with all these partygoers looking on he was supposed to disagree with Jeff and say that he *didn't* want to kiss Annie?

Both the rock and the hard place pinched like hell. "What's the big deal about one kiss?" he murmured to Annie. He took her hand in his—her fingers were almost insultingly cold—and drew her beside the wall Jeff indicated.

While the other man fiddled with the video camera, Annie looked up at Griffin and spoke through her teeth. "I don't want to do this," she said. "I feel...silly."

With his forefinger he notched her chin an inch higher. "Better silly than a party-pooper."

"Go ahead guys!"

At Jeff's command, Griffin obediently bent. He focused on the soft pink of Annie's lips and tried gauging just what kind of kiss it would have to be. Short enough to maintain their dignity, but long enough to prove her desirability, he thought. Annie wouldn't thank him for making it appear he wanted to get it over with.

As he closed in, she let out an almost panicked rush of breath. It puffed mintily against his mouth and mingled with that cinnamony scent of hers. He cupped her shoulders with his hands and felt her stiffen. "Relax," he whispered, then brushed his lips against hers.

She tasted sweet, but she kept her lips primmed and stiff as he brushed by them softly again. Griffin gave a mental frown. At this rate they'd win the prize for best *boring* kiss.

Damn it. Male pride made him want to avoid looking as if he'd lost his touch with women. And didn't Annie claim she'd come here as a seeker of love? Well, no one of the opposite sex would be seeking either one of them back if they didn't demonstrate their ability to provide a halfway decent kiss.

Telling himself it was for the good of all concerned, Griffin mentally donned his best ardent weaponry. Then he slid his hands from Annie's shoulders to Annie's back to gather her closer against him. Her brown eyes widened but he didn't let the surprise in them stop him.

Instead, he hauled her against his chest and bent his head to kiss her. No gentle brush, no shy peck, but a his-hard-mouth-to-her-soft-lips kiss.

Crack.

Griffin couldn't tell if what he suddenly felt was lightning, or the jolt of his heart slamming against his chest wall, or the whole damn house falling down. He didn't care. Whatever it was, it was shocking and strange, yet it still took second place to the startling, delicious sensation of Annie's mouth under his.

There was that minty taste again, that faintly cinnamon scent, and when he pressed harder her mouth parted and he could touch the soft inside of her lower lip with his tongue. She inhaled sharply, drawing his tongue farther inside, and Griffin closed his eyes.

Nothing was this sweet, this hot. Annie's taste rushed through his blood like caffeine, like adrenaline, a high that was part heat and part excitement and Griffin pressed deeper into her mouth. She went boneless and he turned their bodies so that she leaned against the wall and he could lean into the warm, soft curves of her body.

Her mouth opened wider and she made a needy, greedy little noise. Spurred by the sound of her desire, Griffin almost pushed his hips against hers.

Almost.

Because then he remembered where they were, and why they were here, and worse yet, why they were kissing.

He lifted his head, not letting himself take in the expression on Annie's face, and looked over his shoulder, right into the eye of the video camera. "There," he said, pasting on a challenging grin. "Beat that."

Thank God they'd arrived at the party a bit late. There was dancing already in the next room and keeping Annie in front of him, Griffin quickly guided her away from the front door and into the middle of the dancers. Luck was on their side, finally, because it was a slow song, too. With another prayer of thanksgiving, he pulled her firmly but gently into his arms and started moving, keeping her body close enough to hide what that kiss had done to his, but far enough away that his embarrassing condition might have a chance to subside.

He inhaled a long breath. Two. Five.

Then he looked at Annie. Her face was expressionless and her eyes were open in a semi-catatonic stare. "Blink," he said.

She didn't.

"Blink," he urged again.

She finally did and the action roused her attention.

Her gaze lifted and she focused on his face. "Um," she said.

"Exactly," Griffin answered grimly.

He watched her swallow and a flush rose from her cleavage up her neck and over her chin. "Griffin," she said urgently, then she paused. "Um," she said again.

He sighed, then nodded. "I know. But don't worry about it."

"Um?"

He nodded again. "I promise. It'll be okay."

That seemed to soothe her. Her gaze dropped to his shoulder and she appeared to relax.

It *would* be okay, Griffin promised himself. Whatever insane line-up of the planets responsible for that incredible kiss would pass. Had probably already passed.

It didn't matter, anyway. This was a protective impulse good for one night only. Once the party was over, so would be any opportunity for inappropriate actions or responses. He'd already resolved to let her go.

"Griffin?"

He looked down at Annie who now appeared completely recovered. With gentle hands he eased her a little farther away from his body, wishing he could say the same about himself. "What?"

"You don't need to worry about it either."

"I'm not worried." *Yeah, right.* But he wasn't. Because it was o-v-e-r as soon as they left the party. Hell, they were both busy people. His number-one priority was work and always had been. Even though they were neighbors, he'd likely never see her again.

"Well, it makes me feel better to know what happened," she said.

"Other than that the video camera started smoking?"

Even when she frowned, that dimple of hers winked for a moment. "I mean I know *why* it happened."

He knew why. Chemistry. Yin plus yang equaled pow. Somewhere along the line little Annie Smith and Griffin Chase had sipped from the same beaker in Dr. Frankensex's lab. But as they were two different people who wanted two different kinds of lives—she was seeking *love*, while he'd never be good at it—the farther apart they stayed, the better off they'd be. "Go ahead and tell me," he said anyway. "Why did it happen?"

"The robbery," Annie said. "It knocked me for a loop."

"I know, honey." The endearment slipped out.

"I didn't sleep last night."

"That would make anyone act a bit loopy," he agreed.

That little crease between her brows was back. He hated that. She bit her bottom lip. "You see, this thought started nagging me. I have the feeling I *know* the person who robbed the bank."

Griffin stilled. His body, his blood, his heart. *"What?"*

"I just have this weird notion I know him. Though I can't think why and I can't for the life of me think

who it would be.'' Her eyelashes rose and she hit him
with the full force of those big, chocolate-dark eyes.
''But he stopped and stood over me with that gun. I
think it's because *he* knows *me*.''

An icy finger scraped down Griffin's back. Re-
gardless of his body's reaction, he couldn't help himself from gathering Annie tight against his chest. Suddenly he wanted to be ten feet tall. Ten feet wide. A
box made of steel that he could lock her inside.

She thought an armed bank robber knew her. She
thought she knew him.

Hell. That made one thing perfectly clear. Someone
was going to have to look out for Annie Smith. And
even though he was too busy and she was too tempting, for the sake of his sanity it was going to have to
be Griffin. Not for forever—but for a while.

Chapter Four

Monday morning, after visiting her favorite produce stand for a flat of early strawberries, on impulse, Annie stopped by her mother's apartment. It didn't take an Einstein to figure out she wanted a bit of the familiar after the topsy-turvy events of the past few days.

Dropping into the rocking chair in the living room, Annie breathed in the lavender scent that she so closely associated with her mother, and then let the air out slowly. She heard the clatter of her mom making tea for them in the kitchen and let her gaze wander about the room.

How very familiar it was. The furniture was arranged in nearly the same pattern as it had been in the cottage. As usual, framed snapshots stood on the small gateleg table to the right of the window. They showed Annie in various stages of childhood and there were two photographs of her parents. One had been taken on their wedding day. Her parents had eloped, and her mother wore a ruffled paisley dress and her father an embroidered shirt with jeans.

Another photo was a head shot of her father. Annie looked at him closely, idly wondering what had sent this man running away from his wife and young daughter. She'd wondered about it before, of course, but today it struck her as even stranger that her mother displayed photographs of him at all. He'd left her almost twenty-one years ago. Why hadn't she put them away?

"I want to hear all about your Valentine's evening." Natalie bustled in with the tea, and Annie jumped up to help her with the heavy tray.

She carefully set it down on the coffee table as her mother sat on the nearby couch. "It was fun," Annie said, avoiding her mother's gaze as she poured two cups of steaming, clove-scented tea. "Very nice."

Her mom's eyebrows rose as she reached for the teacup and saucer Annie held out to her. "That's all? Fun? Nice?"

Confusing. Surprising. Before the party, looking at her reflection in the brand-new clothes, she hadn't felt like herself. And then Griffin had arrived and the strangeness had turned downright Cinderella-ish. But she couldn't tell her mother that.

She cast about for something harmless to report. "They had games and prizes at the party."

Her mom took a sip from her cup. "Oh, that does sound like fun. Did you win anything?"

"Well, um." Annie stalled by blowing across the

surface of her tea. "An overnight at that new resort outside of town. One of Jeff and Cathy's friends works there—the Strawberry Bay Spa." Annie blew again, hoping her mother wouldn't ask how she'd come to get that prize. The grand prize.

The overnight was for one of the spa's suites and she and Griffin had also won a generous selection of spa services. The certificate announcing the award had been accompanied by a home-made trophy of Valentine Barbie and a tuxedoed Ken glued to a heart-shaped wooden base. The dolls had been face-to-face, standing close. Very, very close. Hand-lettered on the base were the words Hottest Kiss.

Annie closed her eyes, trying to suppress the vivid memory of Griffin pressing against her, his body, his mouth. He'd teased the inside of her lower lip with his tongue, and that liquid warmth had started rising and falling inside her again. Annie's heart stuttered, and, nearly able to smell his intoxicating fragrance, she gulped the too-hot tea, hoping it would burn away the remembered sensation.

"Annie?"

Annie started, then opened her eyes, looking into her mother's puzzled face. "What, Mom?"

"I asked if you met anyone interesting."

"Griffin took me." Annie instantly cursed herself for blurting it out. "Wasn't that kind of him," she added, just to make sure it didn't sound like anything more than that.

Her mother's eyes went wide. "Griffin?"

Annie felt a flush crawl up her neck. "You know. Griffin Chase."

"Oh, Annie." Her mother's saucer and teacup

clacked against the coffee table as she set them down. "Not Griffin."

Annie studied the painted yellow roses sprinkled over the fat belly of the china teapot. "Is that really so bad?"

"I don't want to see you get hurt, Annie."

She frowned. "Mom, I'm not fourteen years old anymore. We went to a party together. As friends. Nothing more. I don't expect anything more."

Her mother reached for her tea again. "It's just that…"

"That I mooned over him for years. That I'm the housekeeper's daughter and he's the man in the big house. I know, Mom. But I certainly wouldn't embarrass myself or Griffin by dreaming that a girlish wish could come true."

It would be really dumb to think there could ever be anything between her and Griffin, for those reasons she'd just expressed. Not to mention that she also knew, thanks to all those years spent mooning over him, that he wasn't the type to settle on just one woman.

Annie looked Natalie straight in the eyes. "Honest, Mom. I'm over all that."

As for last night's kiss, well, she'd get over that, too. Any minute now.

Eager to change the subject, Annie looked around the room and her gaze snagged on a brightly colored postcard propped on the end table beside the couch. "What's that?"

Her mom reached over to nab it then passed it to Annie. "Just more of your aunt's not-so-subtle persuasion. She sends me a new postcard every few days.''

This one showed a bright blue sky, a golden beach and a darker blue bay. Boats with red, yellow and white sails were caught mid-dash across the water. ''It looks great, Mom. You should think about moving to Aunt Jen's in San Diego.''

But her mother was already shaking her head. ''I'm staying put,'' she said.

Unsurprised, Annie looked around the familiar, comfortable living room, once again intensely aware of that sense of waiting in her mother's life. It made her so antsy that for the first time in memory Annie rushed through her tea and left her mother's apartment, excusing her hurry with the—true—statement that she had a lunchtime catering job at the Strawberry Bay Auto Park.

Annie's cell phone rang as she was heading across town toward home. She needed to pack up the sandwiches, salads and cookies that she would deliver to Louis Delvecchio's car dealership. Every month she catered a lunch meeting for his sales staff.

She flipped on her phone as she reached the red light at a busy intersection. As she braked, her car made its usual rough and rumbly idle. ''Hello? Hello?'' It was always hard to hear her cell calls when her car was running.

''Is that you Annie?''

Griffin. The memory of that riveting touch of his warm, wet tongue pressed to the inside of her lower lip burst in her mind once again. Annie gulped. ''It's me. Sorry. I can't hear very well. My car is doing its belch-and-bellow routine.''

"Ever think about getting a new one?"

A million times. But she'd been waiting for...for what?

"Maybe I will," Annie said slowly. She'd bought the staid sedan from her mother and it had been ten years old then. Perhaps it was time she traded it for something young and snazzy.

"I could help you pick out a new car," Griffin offered. "With four doors, air bags and anti-lock brakes. Something reliable and trustworthy."

Reliable and trustworthy didn't sound anywhere close to snazzy. "I was thinking of a car with a little more style." She remembered the wind on her face the day Griffin drove her home. "A convertible maybe."

"A convertible?" He laughed. "What would you want a car like that for?"

Annie sniffed. "Because I have a staid and dependable van I use for business purposes. I want to have something...flashy for other times."

"Flashy?" There was a wealth of doubt in Griffin's voice.

The stoplight in front of Annie turned green and she pressed on the accelerator, her car coughing painfully as it rattled forward. "I definitely need to replace this clunker," she murmured. "With something *exciting*," she added emphatically.

There was a moment of silence and then Griffin smoothly segued the conversation. "Maybe we can talk about it when we visit the spa. Have you checked your calendar yet?"

Annie's stomach lurched. "I thought we settled that last night." Once they'd been awarded their prize, she'd told him immediately that she was *way* too busy to take time off for a weekend getaway.

"Right. You said you were busy and I asked you to double-check your calendar."

"Well, I did," she lied. "I'm busy. Every weekend. All weeks. All year."

Even over her car's throaty rumble she could hear his laugh. "And here I was believing you actually meant it when you said you wanted to be a...seeker."

Annie made a face. "I did mean it." An image of her mom's living room popped into her mind. The same arrangement of furniture, the same pictures, the same, the same, the same. Always that sense of waiting. "But what does that have to do with a visit to the spa?"

"I thought we could make a reservation for midweek so it won't interfere with your weekend catering jobs. This Wednesday would be perfect."

Annie blinked. He had this way of announcing things when she least expected it and then she'd find herself going along. It was why she'd let him drive her away from the police station on Friday and why she'd agreed to have him escort her to the party the night before. "Day-after-tomorrow Wednesday? I can't do that."

"Why not?"

"I—" No. She couldn't say, "I don't know." But the truth was that after today she didn't have another catering job until the weekend and she had already prepared most of what she needed for that. "Don't you have to work?" she asked.

"I have a whole department of people waiting on

my reports." He hesitated. "But what's another day or two?"

She stalled, trying to come up with a convincing excuse. "You said *this* Wednesday?"

"I made a call to the spa, Annie. Wednesday is their Singles' Day. They have several activities scheduled to allow single people to meet one another. It could be fun."

Annie bit her lip. "You think so?"

"It's a day made for people like us. I'm back in town after two years and am just as anxious as you to put my social life together."

Annie didn't believe for a second that Griffin needed to go to a spa on Singles' Day to get his social life together, but the truth was, she probably did. Living alone on the Chase estate and catering parties instead of attending them meant she didn't have a multitude of opportunities to meet people. To meet men.

"You could go by yourself," Annie said, still unwilling to commit. "Or with a...with a friend."

"Are you kidding? I couldn't do that to you."

Annie didn't want to admit she was glad to hear that. "You wouldn't be doing anything to me."

"But I would. We won that award fair and square, Annie, and I think we need to share it fair and square, too."

Like they'd shared that kiss. That surprising, heated kiss. The memory of it flamed against her lips, her tongue, like an unsuspecting bite of something jalapeño-hot.

Afterward, she'd claimed the passionate kiss was due to that niggling sense of recognition of the armed robber. The reason seemed even more of an excuse, now, with the kiss's memory still blazing against her mouth.

Annie braked at the next stoplight and tried to think the whole thing through, but her car was shaking so badly it made her teeth rattle, and *that* made her only think about how she'd been waiting to buy a better car just like she'd been waiting for everything else in her life.

As she accelerated once again, she passed a branch of the Strawberry Bay Savings and Loan. It wasn't her branch, the one that had been robbed, but it was like a slap on the behind all the same. She wanted to change her life, and that required seizing opportunities as they came.

"I'll do it," Annie told Griffin. "I'll go with you to the spa on Wednesday."

Despite her agreement, however, by the time Annie had rattled home in her car and was loading up her van with the food for the lunch at the auto dealership, she again experienced some very serious doubts about a night away with Griffin.

As she passed the Chase home on her way out of the estate, she braked her van. Her gaze ran over the house's magnificence, her insecurities mounting. With its windows gleaming and fretwork freshly painted, the home was as fairy tale-ish as the idea of Annie and Griffin together. She was the house-keeper's daughter. He was the elder son of the Chase family.

Of course, their spa visit wasn't intended as time for them to be *together* together. But he'd been the boy and then the man she'd watched from afar for years. Did she really want him around, witnessing, assessing even, while she pursued a romantic life? It made her feel awkward and self-conscious just thinking about it.

She was still agonizing over the idea as she steered her van beneath the portico of the Delvecchio dealership's sales office. It seemed from out of nowhere a man materialized in front of her. She gasped, her foot slamming on the brake.

Heart pumping at emergency level, Annie jerked off the ignition and hopped out of the driver's seat. "Joey!" she managed to get out. "You scared me to death."

Dark-haired Joey Delvecchio, nephew of the dealership's owner, Louis, looked a bit nervously pale himself. "Uh, sorry, Annie."

She'd known Joey since Miss Benton's kindergarten class at Strawberry Bay Elementary. Both of them painfully shy, their teacher had paired them as the paste-and-scissor monitors for the entire year. Usually, the sight of Joey made her think of the soapy smell of sticky paste jars.

Today—today she couldn't stop thinking of how he'd just startled the socks off her.

Inhaling a deep, calming breath, she mentally shook her head and dredged up a smile. Joey's expensive-looking sports jacket, slacks and polished loafers indicated he was doing well selling cars. So much for the shy scissors monitor. His bashfulness must be a thing of the past.

"How are you, Joey?" She walked around to the back of the van and opened the double doors.

"Great." He followed her over to help her slide

out two large wheeled coolers. "Business is really, really great."

"Yeah?" She pasted on that smile again as he grasped a cooler's handle and started rolling it toward the door leading into the conference room. "I'm glad to hear that."

He held the door for her so she could pull the other cooler through and then he followed her into the air-conditioned room. Three walls were hung with whiteboards covered with multi-colored graphs. The pungent smell of dry-erase markers lingered in the air.

Joey opened his cooler and started passing to Annie the containers inside. She, in turn, arranged them on the long conference table. "Thanks for the help, Joey," Annie said, ignoring her still-jittery pulse. The memory of handing out kindergarten supplies resurfaced. "Kind of reminds me of old times."

He kept his gaze on the contents of the cooler. "I heard what happened to you."

Annie grimaced. "The bank robbery?"

"No." Joey fumbled inside the cooler for the next container. "Uh. Well that, too. But I meant I heard about the Valentine's Day party. That you won the grand prize."

"Oh." Even in the frigid room, Annie felt her cheeks heating up. She'd never been the victim of the town grapevine before, though she'd gleaned plenty from it herself over the years. "Yeah. Well. Lucky me."

"Really lucky." Joey nodded. "The Strawberry Bay Spa. I've been there a few times myself since it opened. I'm thinking of buying a couple of weeks in one of their time-share condominiums."

"Oh, yeah?" Annie looked at him with new interest. Word was that those time shares were going for a pretty—pretty pricey—penny. Shoot, if Joey Delvecchio could conquer his shyness enough to sell strangers cars, and sell them successfully enough to not only have a classy wardrobe but buy a time share at a posh resort, then how could she be such a coward? Surely she could co-exist with Griffin for a day-and-a-half.

"I'm impressed at what you've accomplished." Annie said. "What's your secret, Joey?"

His fingers slipped on the edge of the cold-cut tray he was holding out, but Annie managed to save it from hitting the ground. "My secret?" he echoed.

"To your success." Annie clarified. "I'm still battling the bashfuls, I guess."

He was silent a moment. "Taking chances," Joey said. "Not being afraid of something…exciting."

Annie nodded. "I know you're right, of course." She bent to open the second cooler. "Chances. Something exciting. Hmm." It was nothing she hadn't been telling herself dozens of times over the past few days. Several times already *today*.

On a sudden, inspired thought, Annie looked up. "Hey, Joey. I'm thinking about replacing my car. Do you have anything you could sell me? Not too expensive, of course, but not boring either."

Joey appeared surprised, but then his face lit up. The small smile he wore reminded her of that shy scissors monitor all over again. "I think I have just the thing."

Griffin didn't consider himself an interfering man. He saved his energy, opinions and judgments for when they could improve or expand Chase Electronics. In his personal life he was careful to keep his thoughts to himself.

He'd never presumed to discuss with his father how his single-minded focus on the business had resulted in an almost forty-year-long union that didn't appear to make either one of his parents particularly happy.

Griffin wouldn't dream of broaching with his brother Logan the subject of the almost-engagement that he'd been sitting on for a decade. Not even when the two of them were ending a long day at the family company with a six-pack of beer and a double order of rolled tacos from their favorite corner taco stand.

Live and let live, Griffin always said.

At least he *would* have said that, until the sassy *toot* of a car horn had had both him and Logan jumping out of their skins as they headed up the front steps to the house.

They turned, but the only things to see were the flash of a red bumper and red taillights disappearing in the direction of Annie's cottage. "Who the hell was that?" Griffin demanded.

Logan shrugged. "Annie?"

"No." Griffin refused to believe it. He didn't *want* to believe it. Logan's contact at the police department had said they didn't have any good leads about the bank robbery Annie witnessed or any of the previous ones they suspected were perpetrated by the same person.

Put that together with Annie's feeling she and the robber knew one another, and his blood chilled at the idea of her dashing about town in something red, in something that *tooted* for God's sake, drawing attention to herself. "We better go check this out," Griffin said to his brother.

Logan stared. "What's going on? Why have you suddenly elected yourself her keeper?"

Keeper. Keeping Annie. In all honesty, Griffin couldn't deny it. Keeping her safe was his hidden reason for insisting on the almost immediate midweek visit to the Strawberry Bay Spa, despite all that needed to be done at Chase Electronics. It gave the Police Department some more time to solve the case with Annie safely out of circulation.

"Someone's got to look out for her," he told Logan. He trotted back down the steps, not waiting to see if his brother followed.

Logan was grumbling behind him. "I'm only coming after you because you have the food."

His brother grumbled even more once they reached the cottage—a midget-sized convertible parked on the gravel space beside it—when the person who opened Annie's front door was her friend Elena.

"You!" Logan said.

After a minute, a playful, yet not-really-friendly smile broke across Elena's face. She was really a very pretty young woman, Griffin thought. "Annie!" she called over her shoulder and sniffed appreciatively. "A couple of delivery boys have brought our dinner!"

Elena sniffed again and her smile was only for Logan this time, and rapier-sharp. "Mexican? I wouldn't have thought it was something *you* liked."

"I like it just fine. I *liked* it just fine. Too much maybe." Logan said through his teeth.

Griffin looked from one instant and obvious combatant to the other, then shrugged. "That's right. I believe you two know each other."

Elena's dark eyebrows rose. "Oh, I know his kind, all right."

At a loss, Griffin opened his mouth to ask if they could come in, but his brother was already pushing past him. "What's that supposed to mean?" Logan hissed.

Elena stepped back, then turned away and strode into the small living room. "Nothing," she retorted. "Nothing at all."

Logan looked frustrated, yet followed her anyway. "Just what I thought."

Shaking his head, Griffin trailed them, but was distracted from the Logan-Elena mystery conversation when Annie appeared from the direction of the bedroom. "Griffin," she said.

In a pair of sneakers, tight, washed-out jeans, and a T-shirt, she was all at once both four years old and twenty-four. Griffin felt both protective and...possessive. Her big brown eyes blinked, and he remembered all over again her gaze on him, stunned, after that powerful, prizewinning kiss.

He sighed. She was so damn much trouble.

"What are you doing here?" she asked.

Elena shook off the hand Logan had on her arm and walked toward her friend. "Didn't you hear me? It appears that Griffin and..." she snapped her fingers "...Logan, isn't it?...have brought us dinner."

Annie blinked again, though Griffin didn't know if it was due to the unexpected dinner or the unexpected animosity in her friend's voice. "Dinner?"

It occurred to Griffin that he couldn't just barge into a woman's house and start criticizing her choice of cars. "Sure. Yeah. Dinner," he said, holding up the bag of tacos.

Logan groaned loudly. "Do we have to—"

"Share?" Elena snagged one of the beers from the cold six-pack Logan held. "Absolutely. As hard as it may be for you to believe, I really don't have cooties. Or anything else catching."

Griffin could have kissed Elena—though he wondered if that might have made his brother even angrier—because within minutes she'd directed the four of them to the scarred kitchen table and had passed around plates and napkins.

Annie still appeared slightly stunned, but her expression turned immediately suspicious once he brought up her new car. "What do you mean, you don't like it?" she demanded.

He shifted in his chair. "It's not that I don't *like* it, Annie. I just wondered…if you'd thought it through. It's a big purchase."

"And this is your business because…?"

Damn good question. It wasn't any of his business and he actually assumed that Annie was smart enough to make a savvy deal. But Annie and that little red car would attract every eye in Strawberry Bay… including an armed robber's.

He swallowed, unwilling to scare her with the thought. "It's none of my business what kind of car you buy, of course."

She looked slightly appeased. "Anyway, I bought it from Joey Delvecchio at the Strawberry Bay Auto

Park. As a matter of fact, it was his. He gave me a very good deal.''

Griffin frowned. ''Joey Delvecchio of 'I'll eat a kitchen sink of spaghetti to make you a deal at Delvecchio's'?''

''That's Louis. Joey is his nephew.''

''Tell me you had a mechanic check it out, then. And not a mechanic at Delvecchio's.''

Annie rolled her eyes. ''Yes, I had a mechanic check it out. Are you always this bossy?''

No. That was the thing. He was never this bossy. Or this focused on rescuing a woman. As a matter of fact, it had always been his *lack* of focus on a woman that had gotten him into trouble.

''Because if you are, I don't think we should go to the spa after all,'' Annie continued.

He was suddenly glad that Elena and Logan had yet to call a truce to their verbal sparring. Even now they were snapping at each other, totally engrossed in their own conversation. Griffin didn't feel like explaining to his brother the urgency he could hear in his own voice. ''C'mon, Annie. We need to use the prize or your friends' feelings will be hurt.''

She frowned. ''We can give it back to them.''

''But I want to go.''

Her eyes narrowed. ''Yeah, right.''

''I do.'' It was true. He wanted to take Annie away from the streets of Strawberry Bay. He dug around for more words to convince her. ''Remember, it's Singles' Day. Don't forget that you're, um, seeking.''

She pursed the lips of that sweet, soft, distracting

mouth. "You're not going to do all this big-brother stuff when we're there, are you?"

"Big-brother stuff?" He just wanted to make sure she was safe. "Absolutely not. We'll stay out of each other's way. You won't even know I'm there."

Chapter Five

Wrapped in a thick, white terry-cloth robe with a strawberry embroidered on the lapel, Annie sat at a table in the sunroom of the Strawberry Bay Spa. She'd already had a facial, a pedicure, and the rose-colored polish on her fingernails was drying as her hands hovered uncertainly over a meager pile of bobby pins.

She bit her bottom lip and peeked once more at the five cards lying facedown on the wooden surface in front of her. Making a decision, she plucked three bobby pins from her pile. "I'll see your two and raise you one." She nonchalantly dropped them on a heap of other silver-colored pins in the center of the table.

Her new acquaintances and fellow spa-visitors, Esther, Gladys, Dorothy and Marian, checked their poker hands again. Marian folded. Dorothy and Esther, too. But Gladys tossed another of her silver bobby pins on the pot, then spread her cards face-up. "Read 'em and weep."

The septuagenarian had two pair, jacks and twos, which neatly trounced the queen-high poker hand Annie had been trying to bluff with. As the other woman scooped the pot toward the rest of her winnings, Annie shared a commiserating smile with the other elderly ladies. "She beat us again."

The three nodded their silvery heads—hence the silver bobby pins. "Gladys wins every week," Dorothy said. She leaned closer to Annie and whispered loudly. "But once she starts crowing about it, I turn off my hearing aid."

Annie laughed. The ladies were so delightful, it hadn't taken much encouragement for her to join their table. She'd wandered into the sunroom in search of a book and a quiet corner, but these friendly women had ignored her initial shyness and insisted she sit in on their weekly ritual of a poker game following their mid-week massages and manicures.

The first thing they'd wanted to know was what brought her to the Strawberry Bay Spa on a Wednesday. Because, no, it wasn't *Singles* Day, Annie had learned very quickly, once she mentioned it.

It was *Seniors* Day.

She would have liked to discuss that little revelation with Griffin, but soon after they'd arrived he had disappeared, as promised. But now, as Esther was dealing out the next hand, she let out a little sigh, her gaze caught on something outside the French doors that led from the sunroom to the spa's lovely grounds.

No. Esther's gaze wasn't caught on some*thing,* but someone. Griffin.

"Would you look at that?" Esther said. "My friends, do you remember men like that?"

The three other ladies followed her gaze and sighed, too. Shirtless and in swim trunks, a towel slung around his neck, Griffin was walking in the direction of the pool and hot tub. "Look at those muscles. Do you suppose he's the new lifeguard?" she asked, almost purring. "Because I think I need CPR already."

Silver heads shook and all the women laughed.

"He's not a lifeguard, he's…" Annie stopped, unsure how to identify Griffin, "…the man I came with. My, uh, friend."

Four silvery heads swung her way and four pairs of wide eyes stared at her in surprise. Then Dorothy made a cute little snort and reached over with an age-spotted but meticulously manicured hand to quickly sweep Annie's playing cards and bobby pins in her own direction.

Annie glanced down at the empty tabletop in front of her. "I'm out?"

Dorothy snorted again. "You're in. The pool, the hot tub, wherever it is your young man is going."

"He's not—"

"He should be," Esther said seriously. "You can't tell me you want to consider a man like that as your mere 'friend'?"

Annie licked her dry lips. "You don't understand. It's not like that between me and Griffin. We're only here because of a kiss, and—"

"A kiss?"

Annie grimaced at her dumb slip. "On Valentine's Day. It was just a game—"

"That's what they all want to think. They say it a lot of the time, too," Dorothy said. "But it's up to us women to ignore their blather and recognize the real truth."

The other ladies nodded in sage agreement.

What real truth? Annie tried once more to convince them she should stay. "But I was having fun playing with you."

Marian rolled her eyes. "Honeypie, you'll have plenty of time for cards with the old biddies when you're an old biddy yourself. But take it from us. We have almost three hundred years of experience around this table and we can tell you that some chances only come around once in life. Now don't flub this one. Go get that man."

"Or at least take the opportunity to determine if you *want* to get him," Gladys said, with more caution. "Good looks don't make a good husband."

Esther laughed. "No, they only make him better."

Unwilling to enter into a discussion about adequate husband qualifications and pretty certain there were no more playing cards coming her way, Annie pushed out of her chair. With the ladies egging her on, she certainly couldn't refuse to leave the sunroom. "Well, I guess I'll just—"

"Go! Go!" Esther waved her off and the others nodded encouragingly.

With reluctant footsteps, Annie headed for the French doors. Once outside them, she looked back, noting that the poker ladies were watching her with avid interest. Sighing, Annie obediently turned in the direction of the pool, then began walking through the lawn- and shrub-covered grounds dotted with the Mediterranean-style bungalows used by the spa's overnight guests.

With luck, Griffin had been on his way to someplace other than the pool. A massage, a sauna, who knew? If she didn't run into him right away, she bargained with herself, she'd make a beeline for their rooms.

Annie didn't like the notion of wasting opportunities, and yes, at some point she wanted to confront him about the singles/seniors mix-up, but hadn't they agreed to keep out of each other's hair? Vividly recalling the hard lean wall of his bare chest and then those muscles rippling from his shoulders to his backside as he walked past the sunroom, she was certain she'd be more comfortable talking to him when he was clothed.

A clay-colored stucco wall covered with scarlet bougainvillea surrounded the pool area. With a deep breath, Annie pushed open the wrought-iron gate and stepped inside. There wasn't a soul in or beside the turquoise waters of the Olympic-sized pool. Okay, so there. She could tell her poker-playing buddies that she'd tried seizing the opportunity, but it wasn't meant to be. Feeling a giddy sense of relief, she took a step back.

"Is that you, Annie?"

The voice directed her gaze to the right of the pool, where a hot tub bubbled under a canopy of slatted wood and more blooming bougainvillea. His darkly golden hair curling on the ends and his wide shoulders dotted with drops of water, Griffin had the steaming water all to himself.

He smiled as if he didn't have a care in the world. "Are you having fun?"

Annie scowled, suddenly annoyed at how good he looked, annoyed that she noticed, annoyed that she was annoyed. The only reason she'd agreed to this little adventure was to put some other man in her mind. But instead, she kept butting up against this one.

And goodness. Even that sounded delicious.

"Annie!" he called out again. "I said, are you having fun?"

She crossed her arms over her chest and stalked toward him. The morning's luxurious treatments had been novel, if not downright decadent, and she'd enjoyed them all the more anticipating the "singles" she'd expected to meet later. But, thanks to him, the only single male she'd met was the one she positively couldn't have. Him.

Her annoyance redoubled. She stopped, eyeing him across the bubbling water. "Tons of fun," she said sweetly. "I met some new people already."

"Oh, yeah?" Some expression—guilt, maybe?—waved over his face.

"Oh, yeah." She dropped to the edge of the hot tub, and hitching up her knee-length robe, nonchalantly dangled her feet in the warm, churning water. "Four women. In their seventies."

His mouth twitched. "Singles?"

"Widows."

His mouth twitched again, then he finally couldn't hold back his crooked grin. "I'm sorry, Annie. I guess I messed up.'' He lifted his hands. ''Singles, seniors? It's a mistake anyone could make.''

Annie narrowed her eyes. There was no reason for him to have intentionally misled her, but all the same, she couldn't shake the feeling that he had. ''You owe me,'' she said. ''I took time away from my business thinking this might lead to something special.''

''I know.'' Another wave of almost-guilt passed over his face. ''But I'll make it up to you, I promise. How about if I buy you a special dinner tonight?''

She frowned and when she opened her mouth to refuse—they were supposed to be steering clear of each other!—he reached into the bubbling water and circled his fingers around one of her ankles.

''Come on,'' Griffin said coaxingly, ''don't be mad. I hate it when I make a woman mad. Just say yes. Let me make it up to you.''

Annie glared at him. No mere touch, no boyish wheedling was going to change her mood. ''Why should I?''

''Because it's no fun being angry with me.'' He smiled disarmingly and, gripping her ankle more firmly, lifted her foot free of the water. ''And because your toes look so…cute.''

Annie froze, trying to keep all ten of them from curling in reaction. She frowned at his oh-so-smooth charm. ''My toes were expecting to meet eligible single men,'' she said.

He brought his other hand into play, sliding the palm against the sole of her foot, caressing the arch with his fingers. ''They're disappointed that the only eligible, single man they get to meet is me?''

Annie didn't think her toes had a thought left in

their little heads. *She* couldn't think, because he was still caressing her. Then he slid his hot fingers up the ball of her foot until the pads of his fingertips pressed against the underside of her toes.

Tingling prickles rushed up her calves, then goose bumps took up the call, spreading to the insides of her thighs. Hoping he wouldn't notice the tell-tale reaction, Annie focused on the hem of her robe, tugging it toward her knees. His fingertips pressed deeper and new goose bumps surfaced on her skin, playing leap-frog with the last set. She cleared her throat. "You're good at that," she said.

He continued his gentle massage. "You think?"

She cleared her throat again. "Sure."

"I can't help myself," he said. "You're nice to touch."

Annie's gaze jumped to his. There was something in his eyes, a struggle maybe, and a heated awareness that she supposed her own echoed. Their gazes locked, his hand moving again on her foot. The tips of his long fingers pressed against her toes, insinuating themselves in the spaces between each one. It was a move at once casual, yet more sensual than anything she'd ever before experienced.

This wasn't supposed to happen, she thought. She wasn't supposed to be attracted to *him,* not when she could never have him. Annie closed her eyes. "Griffin," she whispered.

"Hmm?"

When she lifted her lashes, it was to see his attention focused on his hand cupping her foot, his fingertips so erotically wedged between her pink-tipped toes. There was an intensity on his face that scared her a little, but it was thrilling, too. Her heart pounded.

This was sex, she thought, at once awed and afraid. This was what a woman—even the housekeeper's daughter—found when she ventured out of the corners of life.

The metallic clank of the pool gate opening and closing had Annie jerking her foot away. It landed in the hot tub with a splash as she swung her head to see who had arrived. A couple in their mid sixties walked by, hand-in-hand.

They smiled at Griffin and Annie, and Annie smiled back, raising her hand in a little wave. Unwilling to meet Griffin's eyes just yet, Annie pretended a keen interest in the newcomers.

About thirty feet away, they let go of each other's hand to spread towels on adjoining lounge chairs. The distinctive, summery smell of coconut scented the air when the gentlemen took off his shirt and his wife went about smoothing sunscreen on his shoulders and back.

A gold band winked on the older woman's ring finger and something about her simple, obviously loving movements put a lump in Annie's throat.

"Are you okay?" Griffin asked. "Is something wrong?"

His voice sounded completely calm, completely normal, and Annie wondered if she'd imagined the awareness, the heat, the very sensuality of his touch. After all, he'd known she was mad at him. Perhaps he'd just been massaging her foot as a way to assert friendlier terms. Unsure how to read the situation between them, Annie sat back on her palms, her gaze still on the other couple.

"You'll think I'm silly," she said.

"Let me be the judge of that."

She kept her gaze off him and shrugged. "I'm just admiring that married couple over there," she said truthfully. "I imagine they've been together a long while, but it looks like they still have something…beautiful."

He didn't respond, so Annie finally shifted to look at him. "You *do* think I'm silly." She knew she shouldn't care what he thought, but it made her ache a little inside all the same.

He shook his head. "Not silly, exactly." His gaze flicked toward the older people, then back to her. "How old did you say you are?"

"Almost twenty-five."

He smiled. "I believed in possibilities when I was twenty-five, too. Went looking for them, as a matter of fact."

Annie remembered Griffin looking for possibilities, all right. From her little cottage she'd watched a parade of possibilities—women—march through his life. Well, maybe not a parade, but plenty. She tossed her head. "But now at the so-advanced age of thirty-one you're a cynic?"

"A realist, maybe," he murmured. His gaze went back to the older couple. "Not every marriage is like that one, or how you're imagining that one is, you know. Think of my parents. Can you imagine forty years of *that?*"

Annie swallowed, unsure what to say. She'd lived at Jonathon and Laura Chase's estate almost all her life, and yet she didn't think it was her place to comment on their marriage. "I don't—"

"I *do*. Marriage can just as easily be like the refrigerator my parents call a relationship."

That ache inside Annie turned into a full-fledged hurtful pang. "But Griffin…"

His mouth crooked in something she supposed he thought was a grin. "You're right next door, Annie. Haven't you been watching?"

She shrugged, and then the first thing that popped into her head somehow popped out of her mouth. "I only remember watching you."

He stilled, and it got so quiet she could hear birds chirping over the bubbling hiss of the hot tub. "What? You watched me?"

Annie felt the blush crawl up her neck. "I used to follow you."

He nodded. "I remember."

"When you had your girlfriends over." On the estate, there was that gazebo hidden in the stand of oaks separating her cottage from the house. Griffin had kissed a girl for the first time there…or at least she assumed it was his first kiss. It was the first *she'd* ever witnessed.

"Annie Smith! When I had girls over?" He wore a funny expression, part embarrassed, part something she couldn't name. "You little snot."

"Snoop," she corrected.

He shook his head. "Where?…"

"The gazebo."

He blinked, and she thought maybe a flush was crawling up *his* neck. "When?"

She held up a finger. "You were twelve." She held up another. "And thirteen, and fourteen—"

"Stop!" He groaned, covering his eyes with his hand. "You're going to give me nightmares, Annie, thinking of what you might have seen."

Something crazy and bold inside her, something that maybe was born those minutes she'd spent with her cheek pressed to pine-scented linoleum, gave him an honest answer. "Then we might be even. Because you gave me…dreams."

With his hand still over his eyes, he didn't seem to be breathing. Annie stared at him, afraid of his reaction and afraid of missing it.

"Annie," he finally choked out. Shaking his head, he drew his hand from his face to clutch at his chest. "We're at the spa on the right day after all. I believe you've just aged me fifty years."

Dinner was over and the bill paid. As they sipped the last of their bottle of wine, Griffin continued to remind himself of—and struggle with—his role as Annie's self-appointed protector. He figured his trouble had something to do with their little interlude in the hot tub.

That damned inconvenient chemistry between them had a powerful reaction to hot water. Or maybe it was the butter-yellow dress she was wearing tonight, a dress that looked butter-soft, too, and that brought out the blond highlights in her honey-colored hair. The fabric covered her from throat to wrists to knees, but clung to every curve that emphatically announced that Annie was all grown-up.

Or maybe it was because they had the Strawberry

Bay Spa's dining room nearly to themselves. Apparently the mid-week crowd, the seniors there for the senior specials, were day visitors who drove home in their Caddies and Lincolns after the early-bird dinner seating.

With the soft strains of Glenn Miller's band stringing pearls from the speakers in the corners of the room, with their table's candlelight shining like stars in Annie's eyes, Griffin tried to think of her less as a desirable woman and more as an old friend he was watching over—in an avuncular sort of way. If he could run Chase Electronics, certainly he should be able to run his own life with the same cool control.

For God's sake, it should prove easy. He did feel eons older, not just because of that kiss-watching she'd confessed to, but because of that yearning he'd read on her face when she'd talked of the old married couple by the pool. He shook his head, lifting his glass of merlot. Of course, it wasn't that he was emphatically bleak on marriage. Only on marriage for a career-focused man like himself.

Still, that razzle-dazzle reaction of hers to the older couple was a puzzler. Who could be *that* rosy when it came to a legal state that more than half the time ended in divorce? He thought of his parents and grimaced, the beginnings of a headache pounding at the back of his skull. Maybe marriage should end in divorce even more often.

"Are you all right?"

Griffin lifted his head, focusing on the pretty face across the table. "I was just thinking—"

Annie sneezed. Then again. "I'm sorry." She picked up a stamp-sized purse from the tabletop, opened it, and like a magician, managed to pull from it a large but delicate-looking handkerchief.

Griffin smiled, watching Annie use it to stifle another ladylike sneeze. "Your mother always used to carry a handkerchief. I can't think of another woman I've ever met since who does."

Annie folded the square back into her purse. "I guess it's a family tradition."

Griffin cocked his head, thinking he didn't know any of Annie's family other than her mother. "Are you close to your relatives?"

Annie shook her head. "No. Most of the ones I know about died before I was born. But I have my mother's sister, my Aunt Jen, who retired to San Diego a few months ago."

"What about your father?"

"Gone."

Griffin looked at her hand, relaxed around the base of her wineglass. Without thinking, he covered it with his own. "I'm sorry, Annie."

She looked up at him. "Oh. No. Not *gone,* gone." Her teeth came down on her bottom lip. "Well, not that I know of, anyway, and I'm pretty sure I would. He left my mom and me when I was four. That's why my mom took the job working for your mother and father."

He remembered that quiet, pigtails-with-pink-yarn little girl who'd come into their lives along with the best cookie-baker who had ever flipped on an oven. That little girl's life had just gone through a major upheaval when she'd moved to the estate. No wonder she'd been all big eyes and quiet whispers. "I'm afraid I wasn't very friendly to you."

She smiled a little. "I was very shy."

He narrowed his eyes. "And lonesome?" Living on a big estate with only two older boys who mostly ignored her couldn't have been much fun.

"Lonesome? Maybe." She drew her hand out from under his. "Yes, actually. Always."

Griffin didn't like the way her quiet admission made him feel. While it went some way to explaining her rosy regard of marriage—she probably thought it was a built-in antidote for loneliness—it made him feel like he'd never really *seen* her when she was a little girl. He'd certainly never looked at her like he was looking at her now.

One of the other three couples in the room got up from their table and began moving slowly around the small hardwood dance floor. Another big-band tune was playing and Griffin reached for Annie's hand again. "Dance with me," he said, suddenly wanting to hold her against him.

Her fingers tried sliding out of his, but he wouldn't have it. "Dance with me," he said again and stood up, bringing her with him.

Now it was a cheesy Dean Martin song, something better suited to a Vegas lounge than a semi-deserted chi-chi spa in California, but the music hardly registered. Griffin curled Annie's hand against his chest and breathed in her soft warmth and the strawberry scent of her hair. She always smelled good enough to eat, and he hated that she'd been lonely.

"I hope I didn't…embarrass you," she suddenly said.

He frowned and pushed her a little away to look into her face. "Embarrass me how?"

"When I said I watched you in the gazebo."

"Oh." The truth was, he'd been putting off identifying exactly how he felt about that.

"And I don't want you feeling sorry for me either." Her brown eyes were serious as they searched his face. "If that's what this dance is about."

"No." He drew her tighter against him so that her soft breasts pressed against his chest. "No, I don't feel sorry for you. Maybe I think about that little girl I never really got to know, and regret that, but I'm not sorry for *you*, Annie. The woman you."

Oh, great. That had done it. *The woman you.* He wasn't supposed to be thinking of her in those terms. The women he should be thinking about were those game for some casual, mutually satisfying sex.

"Are you sure I didn't embarrass you?" Annie asked.

He shook his head. "That you watched me, that you…thought about me…. Well, hell, Annie, I suppose I'm flattered."

It was sweet. Alluring, even. Almost as sweet and alluring as the curve of her full mouth that was right this instant turned up toward his.

But before he made a big mistake and took another taste of it, he hastily dropped her hands. "We should go back to our suite, I think."

Annie looked at him with those big, serious eyes again. "You do?"

"Uh-huh. Yes."

She was quiet all the way back. His hands in his pockets, Griffin breathed in gulps of sanity-inspiring cold night air as they walked through the quiet grounds. Their door was in sight, he was even reaching for the key, when Annie finally spoke again.

"I used to stand in the trees and pretend you were kissing *me.*"

Griffin touched the solid wood of the door. He tried thinking solid, protective thoughts. Then he thought of that kiss on Valentine's Day and the way her voice had just now gone all husky and, as he opened the door and held it for her, he couldn't help saying back, "I suppose it's too late to stop pretending and make it real?"

She'd given him the opening, hadn't she? Who would blame him for the remark when it had been such a long time since he'd had a woman. It was in her court now. She could kiss him again...or not.

"As an experiment?" she asked.

"An experiment?" To his own ears, Griffin's laugh sounded hoarse. He closed the door, closing them both inside. "I think we've already experimented. Remember those five flaming minutes of videotape?"

Only one dim light was burning in the living room of their bungalow and as she leaned against the front door, it was hard to read her mood. "We have to have a reason," she said.

An excuse was what she meant, not a reason, he thought. Something to tell themselves that made the idea of them kissing again not quite so dangerous. "We don't have to do it at all," he felt compelled to point out.

In the darkness, he could just discern the little frown between her eyebrows. "I didn't get to meet any single men," she said.

"Ah. So maybe I need to make up for all those acquaintances lost?"

"Maybe," she whispered.

The idea of her with some "acquaintance," kissing some man that she might have met today made Griffin worry…hell, who was he fooling? It made him angry. Jealous, maybe, for some stupid, irrational reason. He stalked toward her. "So you would have brought some man here tonight?"

Her eyes widened as he came closer. "I don't know," she answered. "If he was nice. Fun. Funny."

He stopped just an inch away from Annie. "You would have let him kiss you, touch you, taste you?" Griffin's hands clamped down on her shoulders.

She didn't seem to realize she was playing with fire. Or maybe she *did* want to play with it. She looked at Griffin and licked her bottom lip.

He groaned, bent his head. "I'm only doing this because…because…hell, I have no idea." His mouth took hers, had hers, made it his.

She was the girl-next-door, the neighbor-that-needed-him, the woman he was supposed to be protecting. But she tasted wild and when her soft lips opened beneath his he pushed his tongue into her mouth with a hunger he hadn't felt since—

There was no hunger like this. His hands moved from her shoulders to her hips and he gripped them, jerking her against him, letting her feel what had been aching all night and now was fully aroused and fully in need of sinking into her as deep as he could imagine. Annie was making sweet, reckless little sounds, and her breasts rubbed against his chest as she lifted her arms to encircle his neck.

He crowded her back against the door, pushing his heat and arousal against the cradle of her thighs and she pushed back, welcoming him, as his mouth roughened against hers. Lifting his head for breath, he was only allowed a quick one before she pulled him back down, her mouth taking his this time, her tongue shyly, then more boldly, filling his mouth.

He sucked lightly on her tongue and she writhed against him. Deep in his throat Griffin groaned, and he slid his hands up her sides and around to her breasts. He hesitated briefly, but she made another of those needy little noises and then he filled his palms with her.

Her mouth broke away from his. She stared down at his hands, as if startled to find them on her breasts, but watched as he caressed their delicate, plump little weight. When he ran his thumbs over her hard, pearled nipples, her head came up and she looked into his face, her eyes wide, her pupils dilated.

Griffin wanted to slam into her right then, take her against the door, but instead he fought for his usual control, then won it. Moving slowly, methodically, he pressed against the small, feminine rise of her body at the V of her thighs. Her breath came more shallowly, and she held herself very still as he played with and teased her pretty breasts and continued to push in rhythm against the lower half of her body.

"Griffin…"

He ignored the needy catch in her voice. He ignored her almost bewildered expression and that arousing, sweet breathlessness.

His thumbs brushed her nipples, circled them, as his hips pushed into the cradle of her body. He rubbed her breasts with his palms and rubbed her with his arousal. She was warm and the slight scent of strawberries in the air was heady. The little noises she was making were almost unbearably sexy.

And then, so quickly, incredibly quickly, it started happening. Hell. He could feel a climax gathering in her body.

It wasn't something a man forgot, the feeling of a woman coming apart when he only had his hands on her over her clothes, but with Annie it was something else. Something more. It was fire, a strawberry-scented blaze. It was the sense that something special, beautiful, wonderful was about to bloom in his arms.

A once-in-a-lifetime flower.

He needed to protect this, too, he thought. Nurture it.

"I don't know…" she whispered uncertainly. "I'm not—"

"It's okay." His own need was pounding at him, but you couldn't have given him anything to make him stop this, keep this from her, from himself. He bent his head and spoke gently against her warm, wet mouth. "Go, baby." Then he kissed her hard, his tongue sliding against hers. Stroke, press, squeeze. *Come on, baby. Fly.*

And, as if his unspoken words inflamed her blood, she shuddered against him. As her body's trembling went on and on and on, Griffin held his hands and body hard against her to let her ride out the sensations. When she was done, he gathered her away from the door and against him, caressing her back with his palms.

Finally, she put her hands on his chest and pushed away. ''Griffin...'' she said.

He had no idea what she was going to say.

But she didn't say anything. She sneezed instead. Four times.

Five.

Chapter Six

If Annie hadn't felt so miserable, she would have worked up a real embarrassment. But those sneezes had turned almost instantly into a raging cold that left her with a perfect reason not to talk to Griffin. Not the rest of that night when she shivered with fever in her bedroom at the spa, not the next morning when he drove her back to her cottage at the Chase estate.

Whenever she felt Griffin's gaze on her—and who would want to look at someone who felt so lousy?— she would close her eyes and throw her handkerchief over her face. He was all that was kind and sympathetic as he carried her small suitcase into her house, yet she shut the door on him with another brain-shaking sneeze and an intense relief. Then she fell into bed and succumbed to sickness.

Thank goodness for her mother and Elena who

were able to handle her weekend catering obligations. By Sunday, Annie was still heavy-eyed and weak, but the worst of the cold had been defeated. She was even eating again, and she'd just heated a pot of homemade chicken soup when she heard a knock on her front door.

Just as she touched the handle, the sound of a heavy, masculine *achoo* reached her ears. Not for a moment doubting who was on the other side, Annie stood on tiptoe to peer through the peephole.

Her nose was red and chapped, as were her lips. She knew she was pale. But in a worn pair of jeans and a T-shirt, it seemed the only signs of illness Griffin allowed were a tiredness that darkened his eyes and a weekend's growth of golden-brown beard on his chin.

He looked dissolute. Dangerous even.

And, oh God, that's exactly what he was to her. Over the past few days she'd worked it all out, of course. The proximity to her long-time crush Griffin, the way that the armed robbery had made her wish for things she'd never before experienced, had added up to Annie taking unprecedented action. Surrendering to unprecedented temptation.

But as much as the robbery had pointed out what was missing in her life, she also knew Griffin wasn't the one to fill the gap. Even if it wasn't just a Cinderella fantasy, even if the housekeeper's daughter had a real chance with him, too many women had come and gone from his life. She'd watched it all with her very own eyes, proof positive that he wasn't the type who was interested in a commitment. And the truth was, she was looking for a man to love her, not leave her. Years ago, her father had already taken care of the leaving part.

Another knock rattled her front door. "Annie!" he called out hoarsely. "Are you in there? Are you okay?"

Sighing in resignation, Annie visualized non-threatening, non-sexy creamed tuna on toast then turned the knob. She stared at him, hoping that the blush she felt rising would at least improve her ghostly pallor. "I just heard you sneeze. Are *you* okay?"

"I haven't seen you in a few days and got worried." His voice sounded hoarse and rough. Tired.

Annie cocked her head. "What have you been doing to take care of yourself?"

"What do you mean? I've been working." A soft breeze wafted by and Annie saw him shiver as if it were an arctic blast.

"You're sick, Griffin."

He blinked at her. "I never get sick."

She rolled her eyes. "You know those chills you have? The sore throat? Sneezing? Let me break the news to you. That's called being sick."

He didn't seem to appreciate the knowledge. "I have work to do. I don't want to be sick."

She clicked her tongue in sympathy. "Darn, how inconvenient. Especially when the rest of us have been praying for the chance."

He blinked again. "You're being sarcastic, aren't you?"

"You're feeling really awful, aren't you?" she countered. Sighing, she put her hand on his arm. She couldn't leave the stubborn idiot on her doorstep, not when she knew the elder Chases were still in Hawaii and the household staff was on vacation as well.

She tugged him over the threshold. "I have hot chicken soup. Homemade."

He didn't look as if he felt like eating. Well too bad. She'd make sure he did. "Just aspirin," he said.

"Whatever you say." He'd do exactly as she told him.

And he did. She managed to insist he eat a large bowl of her soup and slices of homemade bread and cheddar cheese. Just to wash down the aspirin, she told him. Then she pushed him down onto the cushions of the love seat and made the sacrifice of allowing him the TV remote control. Thank goodness he fell asleep about three minutes into the whispered golf commentary, and Annie was able to fold his legs onto the love seat, throw a quilt over him, then switch the channel.

She spent the afternoon curled up in a nearby chair, perusing her cooking magazines and dreaming up new menus. Occasionally she glanced over to check on Griffin, who slept heavily. Smiling to herself, she enjoyed the sense of having him at her mercy. At least with him sick and asleep there wasn't any need for the two of them to discuss what had happened that night at the spa.

He looked harmless, cozy even, under the pastel-shaded quilt. She was battling a sudden, wild impulse to do something crazy like paint his fingernails, when he suddenly awoke.

His gaze immediately found her and he stared at her for a moment. "You're up to something," he said.

"No!"

One corner of his mouth kicked up in that special Griffin smile. "I don't believe you."

"I can't believe *you*," she said. "You're feeling better." It didn't seem quite fair, when the very same cold had kept her bed-bound for days.

"Yeah. I told you I didn't want to be sick."

She shook her head. "And you always get what you want." She meant the remark to be humorous, but once the words came out and their gazes met again, it took on a whole new meaning. A sexual meaning.

Tension hummed in the air, she could almost smell the heat of it, like the scent of something on the stove just on the edge of burning. Annie swallowed. She knew what had occurred that night, of course. But never in her wildest dreams—well, *only* in her wildest dreams—had Griffin brought her to that climactic point. Just by looking at him, a ghost of that ultimate sensation, that ultimate pang of pleasure, plucked at her nerves.

She felt another blush trail like fire up her neck. "I guess we'll have to talk about it."

His gaze didn't waver. "You're surprising me, Annie. I thought your innate shyness would mean we'd avoid the whole subject."

She might have tried to, Annie admitted to herself, but he'd come over, eaten her soup, fallen asleep on her couch. The truth was, she'd given him her cold so she supposed she owed him a little honesty, too.

"I had a crush on you for years," she blurted out.

He gave a little smile. "I kinda figured that."

"It was silly."

He shrugged, and the quilt slid off his shoulders. He didn't look so safe and cozy anymore, but like a hard, big man. With an easy movement, he swung his legs off the end of the love seat and sat up. His palm patted the cushions beside him.

She eyed him warily as she joined him, but instead of taking the place he indicated she pressed into the far corner of the love seat.

"It's no big deal, Annie," he said mildly. "You were just a kid."

She narrowed her eyes. "Are you laughing at me?"

He shook his head. "No way. I know how it is. Everyone does. I had a massive crush on Marsha Stanhope."

Annie frowned. "I remember her. The Stanhopes are friends of your family. Marsha was older than you and had big…"

"Hence my crush on her." Griffin grinned, shrugged. "What can I say? I was thirteen."

Annie crossed her arms over her chest. "When you were fifteen you had your way with her in the gazebo."

His gaze jumped to hers and his jaw dropped. "You watched me—"

"Kiss Marsha," Annie said.

He blew out a small relieved breath. "Well, right. But that just proves the point that it's perfectly natural to want to act on those feelings."

The blush on her face burned deeper. "Why do I suddenly feel like I'm in seventh grade and you're the health and hygiene teacher?"

Griffin grimaced. "Sorry. I was just trying to make you feel less uneasy around me."

"Maybe I would if you'd stop treating me like your baby sister," Annie grumbled.

"If I treated you like my baby sister we wouldn't be having this conversation," he said drily.

"Well. Right," she answered, looking away. But she had to make sure he understood. "I'm over it now, though. The crush." It was absolutely over. She'd tasted a bit of those long-ago fantasies and put the whole goofy feeling to bed—er, to rest.

"Of course you are."

Sighing in relief, she propped her feet on the edge of the coffee table in front of her and stared at the fuzzy toes of her slippers.

Griffin propped his feet beside hers, then nudged her knee with his own. "We're okay, then?"

Annie took a deep breath. "Okay."

He leaned his head against the back of the love seat and closed his eyes. Annie thought about suggesting he leave. She should. She should tell him to go home and take a nap in his own bed, but his running shoes were side-by-side with her slippers and his knee was pressed lightly against hers. It was nice. Comforting. Friendly.

She picked up the remote and switched on the TV. Flipping through the channels, her attention was momentarily caught by the vision of a woman slipping on a wedding dress. Darting a little glance at Griffin who appeared to be asleep again, she lingered, watching the program that followed the real-life wedding of a real-life couple.

Several minutes passed. The strains of the wedding march began, and Annie was suddenly startled by Griffin's loud groan.

"Please," he murmured. "Not the wedding march. Can't we watch something like car racing or Sumo wrestling?"

His eyes were still closed so Annie went ahead and made a face at him. "Why do all men hate weddings so much?"

He chuckled. "Champagne. Rice. Frou-frou dresses. What's to like?"

"That's really what bothers you?"

He rolled his head in her direction and opened his eyes. "I was kidding, Annie. I don't mind weddings. Believe it or not, I was the man of honor at a wedding once."

"There is no such thing as a man of honor."

"Sure there is. Like a maid of honor. I stood up for the bride, who is an old college friend of mine. Passed her the groom's ring."

"Oh." Annie found the idea of Griffin as the man of honor touching and sweet and a complete surprise. "I would never have suspected."

He chuckled. "Me neither. The night she asked me, I had a big question for her, too. I had a ring in my pocket and was going to request the honor of her hand in marriage."

Annie stared. "You what?" She had never heard a whisper of such a thing. Of all the women who had waltzed through Griffin's life, she'd never guessed he'd thought of settling on just one. "You were going to propose?"

"Yep. On Valentine's Day. I had decided it was time for a wife and Nicole was my closest female friend."

Annie couldn't believe it. She couldn't imagine the

golden Griffin Chase, playboy extraordinaire, on his knees, *proposing.* "I just can't…can't see it," she blurted, without thinking.

He closed his eyes, as if the discussion bored him. "Because it didn't happen, honey. Lucky for my pride, she gave me her good news first. Actually, I ended up telling her about it a long time later and we laughed. I'd been so wrapped up in my work that I hadn't noticed that she'd fallen in love with someone else."

Still shocked, maybe even downright appalled, Annie couldn't let the subject drop. "But…but…how did you feel about it? Was your heart broken?"

He laughed. "No." His eyes opened, and they were so blue and so…not sad. "Which was precisely why she said she wouldn't have married me even if I'd gotten the chance to pop the question. Smart woman. She already knew what I figured out later. I'm not the marrying kind."

"I don't understand," Annie said, her voice faint.

Griffin laughed again. "I know, honey. It took me a while to get it, too."

The following Friday morning, two weeks after the robbery, Annie drove to her branch of the Strawberry Bay Savings and Loan. She hadn't told Griffin about her plan, even though she'd spoken to him by phone or in person every day since their conversation on her couch.

He was watching out for her. That was pretty obvious. But she sensed they were coming to be friends as well. If he stopped by her cottage on the way home from work, he stayed for the space of one beer and listened while she shared one of her daily frustrations or triumphs. She gave him the same consideration when he told her about the difficulty he and Logan had running the company when their father wanted a hand in every decision from an ocean away. She knew he brought work home with him, too, but he still found time for her.

Who would have thought that the housekeeper's daughter and the man from the big house next door would actually develop a friendship? But if she had to give it a name, that was it. Yet despite their burgeoning camaraderie, she hadn't confided in him her intention to revisit the bank for the first time. She was afraid she'd fail.

It was fifteen minutes past nine and she had a stack of checks on the passenger seat beside her, when she turned her van into the parking lot. The gas-guzzling vehicle, painted a soft peach and emblazoned with the words ''Annie Appeases Your Appetite,'' made her feel more secure on this errand than her fun, flashy convertible. Squeezing her hands on the steering wheel, she passed a convenient parking space in the nearly full lot and drove to the back row, farthest away from the bank's double doors.

She found an empty spot, parked, then tried gathering her courage. *I can do this.* Taking a deep breath, she put her fingers on the door handle.

I can't do this. Her hand fell into her lap.

Annie cursed the heavy pounding of her heart. For goodness sake, she couldn't avoid the bank for the rest of her life. Yet she could still hear the echoing thunder of those gunshots, smell the acrid odor of gunpowder and fear, taste the bile that rose in her throat even now as she recalled the heavy presence of the gunman standing over her.

Something knocked against the passenger window.

Annie shrieked, then swallowed as much as she could of the sound when she spied a familiar face outside her car. It was her friend—how funny, she'd never asked the other woman's name—her friend whose hand she'd held during the bank robbery. Annie leaned over to open the door.

The other woman was once again dressed in a smart business suit, and she gave Annie a tentative smile. "Hi," she said. "I'm Cybill. Cybill Richards."

"Annie Smith." Annie lifted her stack of checks from the seat beside her and gestured with her hand. "Would you like to come in?"

Hitching up her straight skirt, Cybill clambered in beside her and shut the door. Her gaze went toward the bank. "I'm trying to work up my nerve," she said.

Annie smiled. "Me too," she confessed. "I would have thought I'd be over this by now."

"I hope I never get over it."

Startled, Annie looked at Cybill. "Really?"

The other woman grimaced. "Well, I hope I can make myself go back inside. But the experience…changed me. Helped me make a few decisions. That's good."

Unwilling to pry, Annie just nodded, but then Cybill put her hand on Annie's arm. "You helped to change me, too."

"I did?"

Cybill nodded. "I was starting into a full-blown

panic attack when you told me to think about the things I needed to do. Wanted to do. Remember?''

''Sure.'' Annie had wanted better shoes, better bras, a better quality of ice cream. And somebody to love. A man to love her.

''I'm going to have a baby.''

Annie blinked, smiled. ''Congratulations.''

Cybill smiled back. ''Well, not at this very moment, not that I know of, anyway. But my husband and I decided to have children.''

''That's nice.'' Annie liked babies, too.

''We weren't going to have a family. You know.'' The other woman fingered the sleeve of her expensive-looking business suit. ''We have a good life. Good careers. Vacations. Nice…things. I thought it was enough. We thought it was what we wanted.''

Cybill's eyes focused on the bank doors, though Annie could tell she wasn't seeing them. ''But that day when I heard those gunshots, when you, a stranger, reached out to comfort me, such a love welled up inside me. For my husband, for life, for what more we could create together. It was love that I couldn't stuff back inside myself when it was all over. It's something that I have now to give to our child.''

She turned her head toward Annie, and her smile was a little embarrassed. ''Do I sound nuts?''

Annie shook her head, the sting of tears hot in the corners of her eyes. ''You sound wonderful to me. You're going to be a wonderful mother.''

''I think I will, Annie. That day, I lost some of my sense of security, but gained…perspective, I think. Do you understand what I mean?''

Annie slowly nodded. "I think I do. I gained a little perspective about myself that day, too." She didn't question her ability to share her thoughts, her heart with this near-stranger. There was a connection between them that made her confession feel natural. "I have a career, my own business that I'm pretty proud of. But when it comes to relationships with men...well, let's just say I've always been standing in the corners or hiding behind the trees."

"But now you're stepping out?" Cybill asked.

Annie smiled. "Trying, I guess. Old habits are hard to break. My father left my mom and me when I was a little kid. I don't need a session with a head doctor to realize I'm a little rejection-shy. I've been wasting my emotions longing for an unattainable man because he's safe to care about. If he's unattainable, he can't reject me."

Cybill cocked her head. "Is this unattainable man a rock musician or a movie star?"

Annie laughed. "Heavens, no. Gorgeous as one, but he's someone I'm actually acquainted with."

"Married, then?"

Annie laughed again, then sobered. "No. I don't think he's the marrying kind."

Cybill smiled a little. "And that's the goal for you? Marriage?"

"Someday, sure." Then Annie sharpened her gaze. "Why do I get the feeling you're trying to make a big point here, Cybill?"

"Maybe I am." The other woman put her hand over Annie's. "I don't know you really, and I don't want to offend you, but what's wrong with attaining the unattainable, if not forever, for a little while?"

Annie's mouth went dry. "What?"

"I can see from your face when you talk about this man that he means something to you. That you'd get something out of having him instead of merely longing for him."

Annie's eyes widened. "I can't *have* him!"

Cybill shrugged. "Maybe not forever, Annie. Maybe you can't marry him. But you and I both know that forever can be shortened in the space of heartbeat. On a Friday morning, as you stand in line at the bank, your life can change."

Or can end. That's what Cybill didn't say. Not that Annie thought it was smart, or even sane, really, to live convinced every breath might actually be your last. Why would anyone then bother paying the bills? Yet still…Cybill had a point.

Annie stared down at her lap. If she went after something she wanted, went after…Griffin—there, she'd dared to think his name—who knew what other wishes she could achieve?

Not that she could think, at the moment, of any others as dazzling or exciting.

She lifted her head and smiled at Cybill. "You might have a point," she murmured. So what that he'd played prince in her Cinderella fantasies? Why should it matter that she was the housekeeper's daughter or even that she was a small-time caterer and he was hotshot company vice-president? "I'm either a woman or a wuss."

Neither she nor Cybill made it into the bank that morning. But when they exchanged phone numbers and hugs, Annie couldn't consider her attempt a fail-

ure. Not when she chanted to herself *woman or wuss,
woman or wuss,* all the way home.

She liked Griffin. Frankly, he excited her. So why
shouldn't she have another taste of that? Before the
bank robbery she wouldn't have thought to make a
grab for that excitement. But now, with this new perspective, why shouldn't she pursue a relationship with
him, even though she knew it didn't have a long-term
future?

That was Cybill's entire point. Nobody could guarantee they *had* a long-term future.

Woman or wuss, woman or wuss. She kept the
chant going in the back of her mind as she punched
out Griffin's number, then spoke to his secretary at
Chase Electronics. Annie was coming out of the corner with a vengeance.

"Is something the matter?" his voice came on the
line, concerned and demanding.

Annie laughed. "No. I just had a quick question
for you."

She could hear his sigh of relief. "Chocolate chip.
Oatmeal is a close second," he said.

She laughed again. "What are you talking about?"

"My favorite kind of cookie. I was certain that's
why you were calling."

She shook her head. A few days ago she'd asked
him his favorite type of muffins and he'd been ecstatic
when she'd delivered him a fresh batch the next
morning. "Don't press your luck. This isn't about *me*
cooking for you."

"What's up then?"

Woman or wuss, woman or wuss. Annie took a
deep breath, trying to banish all her insecurities. "I

wondered if you'd like to have dinner with me at Tori's tonight?'' See? That wasn't so hard. She'd just asked a man out for the first time in her life, and she'd asked out Griffin Chase. The housekeeper's daughter had done it. She'd get all dressed up in one of those date dresses Elena had helped her pick out and—

''Annie…''

Uh-oh. That wasn't an unequivocal ''yes'' in his voice. It was caution. Worry even. A hesitation that bordered on deep concern.

She tried not to feel insulted. And then she tried not to be disappointed in herself as the woman or wuss question was answered. ''I need a helper.'' She improvised quickly. ''Neither my mom nor Elena are free and it takes two…um, two desserts.''

His voice was a little warmer. ''Two desserts for what?''

''To figure out their special sauce.'' Well, they probably had one, didn't they? ''If I eat alone and order two myself, they'll be suspicious.''

He chuckled and the warm sound had her relaxing. ''Is this some kind of corporate espionage?''

''Well, yes,'' Annie said. ''But I promise you, it's not illegal.''

He laughed again. ''Why don't I trust you?''

Because you shouldn't, Annie thought, as he finally agreed. *Because I don't want your protection or your help or your friendship. Just your passion.*

Chapter Seven

Annie stroked a smidgen of perfume on her wrists, then paused with the heart-shaped bottle in her hand, considering. Should she waste the lovely-smelling stuff—the first she'd ever bought for herself—on a man who didn't want to see her as anything but the girl next door? Staunchly refusing to give up the cause, she put another drop on each forefinger and dabbed the scent behind her ears.

Despite the dessert ruse she'd used to get Griffin to go out tonight, she wouldn't give up hope that he might see her as a real, true date by the evening's end. For mercy's sake there was no way he could deny that an attraction ran between them! Every instinct told her he wasn't the kind of man to have touched her as he had at the spa if he hadn't been at least somewhat aroused.

Picking up her purse and keys, Annie strode confidently to her door. Her plan was simple. She'd step over all his usual hearty friendliness and woo him right into a romantic mood.

Griffin was trotting down the big house's well-lit steps as she drove up in her red convertible. With the windows rolled up and the heat on, the car was plenty warm on a spring night, even with the top down.

Annie smiled at Griffin as she braked beside him. Who wouldn't smile at a man who looked even more gorgeous and darkly golden than usual in a gray suit and blue-as-his-eyes tie?

He scowled back as he opened the passenger door then awkwardly poked one foot into the limited space between the seat and the dashboard. "I hate this car," he grumbled. "This is not a man's car."

Annie refused to take the bait. "Joey seemed to like it."

Griffin edged in his other foot. "Joey must have the legs of a dachshund."

Poor Joey. The legs of a dachshund was unflatteringly apt. But then all thoughts of Joey disappeared as Griffin let himself fall into the bucket seat and Annie gulped a breath of his marvelous scent. It was a fresh blend of shampoo, shaving cream and a hint of his ritzy, sandalwood cologne. A shivery chill of excitement ran though her. A man wouldn't take a second shower for someone he considered a pal, right?

The combination of that cheerful idea and her jittery reaction to him made Annie fumble, and she popped the car's clutch as she started down the long private drive. "Sorry."

"I hate this car," Griffin mumbled again.

He didn't seem to get any happier with it as they headed into town and the trendy Tori's restaurant. "Do you have to toot that goddamn horn at every intersection?"

Annie glanced over at him. "I've honked it twice in ten miles. At people I know who honked first."

He grunted. "I still say it's too flashy."

Annie rolled her eyes. "Is something eating you?"

"What have the police told you?" he asked abruptly.

"Told me?" Annie glanced over at him again. "About the robbery, you mean?"

He grunted again.

Annie stared at him in surprise. "I hate to break it to you, Neanderthal man, but they've told me nothing." It wasn't as if she expected them to discuss the details of an investigation with a witness, for mercy's sake.

He made another one of those caveman, dissatisfied-with-the-world grunts.

Annie frowned. He was obviously in a lousy mood. Maybe she should turn around and tackle Griffin and their potential romance some other day. The sound of a car horn had her glancing around, and when she recognized another of her clients, she defiantly *bee-beeped* in return.

Griffin winced. "Too flashy, I'm telling you."

Annie frowned again, then braked for the long red light at the intersection of Bay Road and Field Street. Tori's was a half-block up, and if she was going to change her mind about this date, now was the time. "Is something the matter, Griffin?"

Though a streetlight shined down on him, his eyes were in shadow, dark and unreadable. "I should still be at work, and you look good." He uttered the non sequitur seriously. "You smell good."

"Oh." Annie bit back her smile. "Thanks." From somewhere deep in her collective-female unconscious came the loud and clear message: now wasn't the time to point out just how unreasonable and nonsensical his answer was. "You, too."

He grunted grumpily again.

Then all the females in all the world that had come before her sent another message, too. *Don't give up.* Biting back another smile, Annie vowed to herself she wouldn't.

Still, she was grateful when they reached the restaurant, and she handed the keys to the valet. Though Tori's had notoriously long waits, Annie had managed to nab a just-cancelled reservation earlier in the day, and they were quickly shown to their table.

He ordered a whiskey and she ordered a glass of wine. Behind the cover of an over-large, leatherbound menu, she blew out a long breath. A little conversation, a little good food, but most of all, a little intimacy, and she thought perhaps she could point the man in the right direction. Toward her.

You look good, he'd said. *You smell good.*

"Annie Smith."

Her name, in a booming male voice, had Annie wanting to slide down in her seat and put the menu over her head. Hadn't she just wished for some intimacy for mercy's sake? Hiding her irritation she looked up. "Yes?"

It was a huge, stocky man with a blond crewcut

and a sort-of-familiar face. He held out a beefy hand. "Dean Grayson. This is really great luck."

For who? Annie thought, shaking his big fingers. "This is my…uh—" she'd be cursed if she used the word *friend* "—This is Griffin Chase."

Dean Grayson made quick work of Griffin's handshake and then turned his attention back to Annie. "Really great luck," he repeated.

Annie raised her eyebrows in polite question.

"And I want it to be really great. The best one yet." Dean grinned. "After all, this is the fourth time."

"The fourth time for…?" Annie prompted.

Dean didn't pick up on the hint. Instead, he tapped his chin with a finger the size of a corncob. "Would you happen to know any strippers?"

While her jaw dropped, it was Griffin who asked the obvious question, even as he rose out of his chair. *"Pardon me?"*

Dean blinked. "Strippers. Women who take their clothes off for money." He looked at Annie and grinned again. "Naturally, I thought a woman in your line of business…"

He trailed off as Griffin closed his hand over his thick forearm. "There's no *naturally* about it, I'm sure you'll agree."

Dean blinked, then looked a bit pained. "I don't understand."

Annie gazed from Griffin's guard-dog-on-the-scent expression to Dean's bewildered face. "Dean, I don't think I understand either." She stood, too, and tried prying Griffin's fingers off the other man. "But I'm

starting to get the idea. Did you want to book a catering job?''

''Yes!'' Dean's expression cleared as Annie was
able to loosen the last of Griffin's fingers. ''It's my
brother's fourth marriage, and this time I want to do
it right.''

''Right?'' Annie echoed.

''My brother's sure this one is going to last, so no
tame stuff this time.'' Dean pointed at her. ''We'll
get you to fix some really good grub and then I'll
book a really raunchy stripper.'' His face lit as an
idea appeared to come to him. ''*Four* strippers. One
for each marriage!''

Griffin had apparently had enough. He clapped
Dean firmly on the shoulder and turned him around.
''I'm afraid Annie can't manage to cater your
brother's bachelor party, Dean.''

The other man looked back at Annie. ''No? You
did the food for my cousin Richard's wedding—I remember seeing you there. It was really great stuff.''

Griffin was moving the huge man away, like a tug-
boat ushering a ship out of port. ''Though she really
thanks you for the compliment, Dean, Annie's
booked. Solid.''

Dean looked at Annie again, but he was several
tables away by now. Annie could still hear the mur-
mur of Griffin's voice though, talking to the other
man like a hypnotist determined to bend someone to
his will. ''Busy. Busy. Busy. And don't even think
of looking her up in the phone book. As a matter of
fact, Dean, forget you ever heard her name.''

The two disappeared in the direction of the bar, and
it was several minutes before Annie caught sight of

Griffin again. He was alone this time, and there was fire in his eyes as he reseated himself across from her. Before she had a chance to talk to him, however, their waiter interrupted and Griffin didn't give Annie his full attention until their orders were complete.

Then he looked at her, that fire close to the surface. "Do you deal with men like Dean often?"

"Oh, relax. He was harmless."

"He wanted you to work a *bachelor* party."

Annie let her smile slip out. "I gathered that."

Griffin rolled his eyes in disgust. "I worry about you, Annie, I really do."

Which was exactly what she didn't want. Ugh. Annie had a sudden urge to track down good ol' Dean herself and bop him on his thick skull. "I don't need you to worry about me," Annie said through her teeth. She fiddled with the white linen napkin in her lap. "I told you before, I can take care of myself."

"Okay. Let me rephrase it then. You don't worry me, Annie. You *disturb* me."

Her gaze jerked up. That sounded more promising.

He was shaking his head. "The idea of you at some guy's bachelor party—"

"His *fourth* bachelor party." Her lips twitched.

Griffin's did, too. "With all that good 'grub' and those *four* strippers." He laughed. "Damn, if I'm not wishing I could get an invitation to the thing myself."

Annie took a breath. Took a chance. "But that idea disturbs *me,* Griffin."

Silence fell, and their gazes met over the small expanse of table. Another jittery chill rushed across Annie's skin and then she wimped out and looked away.

"Annie…"

But whatever he was going to say was interrupted by the waiter with their salads. Coward that she was, Annie determined to keep the rest of their dinner conversation breezy and bright. Later, she told herself, later she would go back to what had almost been said between them.

But Annie found their casual talk over dinner seductive, too. Not in a chills-and-thrills kind of way, but in the way of two people finding their mutual rhythm. *He laughs in all the right places,* Annie thought. That was something special right there, that Griffin understood what amused her and was amused by it as well.

And he listened. Some men—lots of men—didn't do that. But Griffin watched her with steady concentration, not for an opening to start talking about himself, Annie realized, but it was as if he wanted to really *know* her.

For someone who had been lonely a lot of her life, for someone who had watched from afar for years, it was a heady, exciting idea.

When the waiter had cleared their plates and passed them each a dessert menu, instead of glancing at his, Griffin looked at her expectantly. ''Well, what's it going to be?'' he asked.

''What's what going to be—'' Annie halted her tripping tongue. ''Oh! Oh. That sauce. Right. Yeah.'' She'd been so caught up in enjoying his company that she'd completely forgotten the excuse she'd used to get him here.

Biting her bottom lip, she quickly scanned the menu, looking for an item that might do. ''The mocha cheesecake with the raspberry-strawberry sauce," she said, looking up at the waiter.

"Two," Griffin added.

Annie ignored her protesting, very full stomach. "Yes," she said faintly. "Two."

When they came, Griffin edged his to the middle of the table. "All yours," he said conspiratorially.

Annie stared at her own plate. "They certainly serve large portions here, don't they?" Still she gamely swirled the tines of her fork through the sauce dribbled over the cheesecake and then touched them to her tongue.

"Good?" Griffin asked.

Closing her eyes, she savored the flavor. "Yeah." Then she dipped her fork again, and sucked at it to get another taste. "Very good."

Her eyes opened, and she looked at Griffin. His gaze was focused on her mouth. By turns earlier that evening, he had looked grumpy or protective or amused. Now he looked...like he couldn't look away.

Annie's pulse jumped. The light from their table's candle washed up against his face, coloring it softly, limning the edges of his brown hair with golden fire. She'd come here hoping to touch that, hoping to reach out to that golden, romantic dream of her childhood fantasies.

But he was more than just the prize she'd dreamed of all those years, she realized now. He was a man who had his own history and his own demons. If Annie wanted to stop waiting for life to happen to her, if she wanted to really live, she needed to let go of all those one-dimensional daydreams and grow up.

If she wanted this beautiful man to see her as a woman, she needed to act like one.

Tingling with anticipation, Annie leaned forward. She owed him something for this burgeoning friendship and for the more she hoped it could be. "Griffin," she said softly. "I want to be honest with you—"

"Son!"

"Annie."

She looked up, startled to see an older couple looking down on them in equal surprise.

Griffin blinked, obviously surprised, too, and stood up. "Mother." He kissed her cheek, then shook his father's hand. "Dad. I thought you weren't expected back until next week."

Annie hid her disappointment at the interruption and stood up, too. "Welcome back, Mr. and Mrs. Chase."

Mrs. Chase gave Annie one of her serene smiles. "Thank you, dear. How have you been?" If she was surprised to find her son eating dinner by candlelight with Annie, she was too polite to let it show.

"I've been fine." Annie glanced over at Griffin, then back at the older couple. "Did you have a good trip?"

"Couldn't stand all that relaxation," Jonathon Chase said, a small smile breaking the normally stern expression on his deeply tanned face. "Had to get back to work. We were on our way home from the airport and thought we'd stop for dinner."

Annie grasped her fingers together. "Would you—" she spared one last glance at Griffin, but his face was unreadable "—like to join us?"

"Oh, no, dear. We won't bother you—" Mrs. Chase started, but Mr. Chase was already pulling out a chair and sitting down.

"We're almost done, Dad."

"No matter," Jonathon Chase said. "You can go whenever you like."

As if Jonathon Chase had any intention of letting them do anything they wanted to, Annie thought several minutes later. While she and Mrs. Chase exchanged small talk about her trip, Griffin's dad monopolized his attention, grilling him on the status of several projects at Chase Electronics.

Griffin appeared just as absorbed as his father. From the corner of her eye, Annie watched their twin intent expressions. She doubted either one of them remembered she or Mrs. Chase was there. But, as if he sensed her regard, Griffin suddenly shook himself.

He grimaced. "Enough, Dad. We can discuss this another time. We're totally ignoring Annie and Mother."

Jonathon's eyebrows rose in surprise, as if he'd forgotten that the women even existed. But then he smoothly covered his gaffe, and switched his attention, sending Annie another of his small smiles. "Well, little Annie, what are you up to with my son?"

It's not an accusation, Annie told herself, instantly hushing her housekeeper's-daughter doubts. Still, she had an answer ready that she knew Jonathon would understand. She leaned toward him and whispered loudly. "I'm trying to figure out their dessert recipe."

Jonathon Chase laughed in delight. It softened his

face and made his blue eyes light. "A businesswoman after my own heart!"

Mrs. Chase smiled, too. "Something for the anniversary party, Annie? You said you'd surprise us for the dessert."

Annie shook her head. "No, I have another idea for that. We should get together soon to discuss the details, though."

Mr. Chase looked from Annie to his wife. "Anniversary? Details?"

Griffin made an annoyed, impatient sound. "*Your* anniversary, Dad. Ring any bells? Mother's been planning a big party."

Jonathon didn't appear the least ashamed. "A party, you said?"

In a flash, Annie found herself with a clear, unpleasant view of the older couple's relationship. Griffin had hinted at it before, and she'd seen signs of it herself, but now she truly understood. They lived distant from each other. Apart.

She swallowed. "It's going to be quite a lovely event at your house on March twenty-third." Annie didn't want to look at Griffin's mother. "A hundred and fifty guests," Annie continued, trying to feed Mr. Chase the details and smooth the awkwardness away at the same time.

"Fine." With a wave of his hand, Jonathon brushed the party out of his mind. "But that reminds me of those quarterly reports due in April…" The gate was open and he was off, galloping through details of the business once more.

Annie swallowed and turned to Griffin's mother. She expected Mrs. Chase to be perturbed, or at the very least hurt by her husband's inattention, but instead she picked up a menu the waiter had left and opened it, every hair in place, every emotion hidden.

The remainder of the time the four shared the table it didn't get any better. Griffin's father virtually ignored his wife, while she seemed perfectly content to do the same. By the time Griffin broke free of his father's conversation and told Mr. Chase that he and Annie *had* to leave, she had a hornet-sized headache buzzing between her temples.

As Griffin grabbed her wrist and hurried her out of the restaurant, Annie couldn't help but look back. Jonathon and Laura Chase might as well be sitting on different planets for the notice they appeared to give one another.

Once they were back in Annie's car, driving away, Griffin took a long breath of cold night air and pushed his thumbs against his forehead. "Pretty awful, isn't it?"

Annie thought about pretending she didn't know what he was talking about, but then gave up. "Maybe it's just jet lag."

Griffin shook his head. "It's always like that."

"It's…sad." Annie wondered why she'd never really noticed it before. Watching them through their windows, her nose against the glass, maybe she'd thought it was the way rich people did things. Maybe Jonathon and Laura Chase had been merely puppets in her fantasy big house, and she hadn't considered them and their inner lives at all.

Griffin made a weary noise. "God. Forty years just like that. With that distance. That coldness. That single-minded focus on the business. My father should never have married.''

Annie swallowed, something about the bone-deep fatigue in his voice making her anxious. ''Maybe it was different before. Earlier.''

Griffin had his head tipped back against the seat. His eyes were closed. ''Nope. It's been like that as long as I can remember. There's duty there. Obligation. But nothing else.''

Duty and obligation. Emotions Griffin felt toward the housekeeper's daughter? The idea was as cold as the wind slapping Annie's cheeks. She glanced at him. He looked as tired as her heart felt. Her hopes of wooing him into a romantic mood blew away into the dark night.

Late the next evening, Griffin stared at the screen of the TV in the upstairs den. All day he'd wanted to find a spare moment to get over to Annie's and apologize. He'd been a hell of a companion the night before, especially after his parents had joined them at their table. But since the brewing of the first pot of coffee this morning, his father had insisted on going over reams of paperwork. Griffin usually would have joined him without a grumble, but this time he'd almost resented that he and Logan had to spend the entire day and early evening in their father's office at the estate. Jonathon Chase was nothing if not single-minded.

Griffin admired that quality and understood his father's passion for the family business. Through genes or some sort of osmosis, that same passion and focus had led Griffin to spend two years away from Strawberry Bay, working his butt off for Chase Electronics.

But a picture of the kind of marriage a man like his father—or a man like Griffin—could make was just one more thing he wanted to protect Annie from. If he hadn't let his parents intrude on the end of their evening the night before, then she wouldn't have witnessed a relationship such as his mother and father's. Annie Smith, with her sweet face and her rosy view of marriage, didn't need to know what the workaholic members of the Chase family were capable of. No— what they *weren't* capable of.

Griffin closed his eyes. Annie's face sprang into his mind, her expression dismayed as his father made clear he remembered nothing and cared even less about the anniversary party that Griffin's mother had devoted so many hours to.

But then another memory overrode that one. Before his parents interrupted, Annie sucking berry sauce from her fork. Hell, he'd gone hard at the sight, the blood pounding in waves to his groin, as he watched that soft mouth of hers wrap around the utensil. Her eyes had turned dreamy as she'd licked away the last drop. She'd have run if she'd known how hot that made him.

But instead Annie had leaned toward him, and she'd said...

I want to be honest with you—

The words struck him strangely now, because he couldn't guess where they'd been heading.

Suddenly Griffin wanted to know what she'd been about to say.

He pushed out of his leather chair and headed for

the door. He had to pass Logan, stretched out on the matching couch, who earlier had declared himself keeper of the remote and who had proved his worthiness for the position by clicking through the channels with bored regularity.

"Where are you going?" Logan asked.

Griffin stared at his brother. Logan had his own condo—as a matter of fact, it was *Griffin's* condo that his brother had yet to vacate—but Logan hadn't gone home after their long day with their father. "Isn't this Saturday night?" Griffin asked his brother. "Shouldn't you be with Cynthia?"

Logan shrugged. "It's her night for her monthly avocado oil hair treatment, she said."

Griffin stared. Maybe Logan knew what he was doing. Maybe his brother's girlfriend knew what *she* was doing. But Griffin couldn't help thinking that their near-engagement wasn't quite as near as everyone seemed to think.

Shaking his head, he continued toward the door.

"Where are you going?" Logan asked again, sliding his legs off the couch and to the floor.

"I'm going over to Annie's," he said. There was no reason to keep it a secret, he told himself. It was just one friend going over to see another.

"I'll come with you." Logan stood up.

There was no reason Logan shouldn't, Griffin told himself, too, stifling his irritation. Surely he could find a quick moment to apologize to Annie. It wasn't as if there was really anything private going on between them.

They found Annie's cottage dark, however, except for a small light burning beside her front door. Griffin frowned, considering, then went ahead and knocked anyway. So what if she was asleep? He wouldn't get any rest until he talked to her.

When nothing happened, no light switching on inside, no footsteps, Griffin knocked again.

"She's not home, bro," Logan said.

Griffin threw his brother an annoyed look. "Where else would she be?"

Logan turned around and pointed. That teensy, irritating-as-a-fire-ant, *flashy* car of Annie's was coming down the drive. Griffin couldn't think how he'd missed its whiny drone.

Because you were thinking only of seeing Annie again. Griffin impatiently ignored the little voice, then impatiently waited for Annie to arrive at the cottage.

"What the hell was she doing out on a Saturday night?" he asked Logan, as the car came toward them.

But Logan didn't answer, his attention fixed on the woman in the passenger seat. As the car braked to a stop nearby, Elena tossed her sleek fall of dark hair. Griffin could see her convincing Annie to go out on the town and do…something.

"That woman is trouble," he murmured.

"Oh, yeah," Logan agreed quietly. "Trouble. She always has been." Despite that, he slowly walked toward Elena as she jumped out of the passenger seat. She was wearing something red and clinging and Griffin could see his brother's shoulders tense.

"There he is!" Elena called out coolly. "My favorite snob!"

Logan paused a moment, then kept on walking toward her.

Griffin grinned faintly and braced himself for all-out war. But then a scent floated through the air. Seeking another breath of it, he turned his head.

Her eyes doe-wide and her expression questioning, Annie came toward him in the dark. She wore a dark skirt but he could see it was slit up the middle, a long, sexy slit. She wore a dark, tight-to-the-skin top, too, with long sleeves. One of her hands clutched the other shoulder and the posture puzzled him.

"Griffin?" she said softly. She fumbled with the tiny purse she carried, and she had to use both hands to catch it. With Annie no longer holding it together, the sleeve of her top fell away from her shoulder.

It gleamed white and smooth in the moonlit darkness. Fragile.

Something spiked hot and sharp in his gut. A protective instinct. Yeah, that was it. Breathing through the hot, possessive feeling, Griffin stared at her and at what was now obviously an aggressive rip in the fabric.

"What happened, Annie?" The heat was still in his gut, but ice flowed through his veins. He discovered he was still able to run toward her. He closed his hands over her arms, struggling to keep his touch gentle as he pulled her near.

"What happened?" he demanded harshly again, his control unraveling in a rush. "What the *hell* happened?"

Chapter Eight

In the moonlight, Annie took in Griffin's thunderous expression. "It's not what you think," she said hastily. His hands were like vises on her upper arms. She'd never seen him so intense. Intent.

She licked her suddenly dry lips. "Or at least what I think you think."

Elena came closer, her temper obviously simmering at the surface as it always did whenever Logan was around. "Hey, Incredible Hulk, relax."

Griffin didn't take his gaze off Annie's face. He gave her the tiniest of impatient shakes. "Not until I know how Annie's clothes were ripped."

"It was nothing," Annie said. "We went dancing and when my partner grabbed my wrist to turn me—"

"I told her there must be a reason there were fourteen of those tops on the clearance rack. Just because we were at the department store, it doesn't guarantee quality,'' Elena continued, shaking her head. ''But would she listen to me?''

Annie shrugged and half smiled at Griffin. ''Defective stitching, I guess. Who knew?''

''Dancing, Annie?'' His hold on her didn't relax. ''You went dancing? Was that—'' He seemed at loss for the right word. ''—safe?''

Elena frowned. ''Safe? Safe from what? A falling disco ball?''

Annie stared at her friend. Really, the Chase men didn't bring out the best in her. ''Elena…''

Elena crossed her arms over her chest. ''What business is it of his? Why does he care where you were tonight?''

Annie looked at Elena, looked at Griffin's tense face, felt the heat of his hands on her arms. ''Yes,'' she said softly. ''Why do you care?''

''I'll tell you why—'' Elena started hotly.

Logan grabbed her elbow. ''Hey, Ms. Busybody.'' His gaze was fixed—bravely, Annie thought—on Elena's snapping eyes. ''Maybe Griffin and Annie don't need you in the middle of this conversation.''

As might have been predicted, Elena instantly turned on Logan. ''*Busybody?* What gives you the right to call me names?''

He tugged on her elbow as he backed away from Annie and Griffin. ''*Snob?*'' Logan appeared to think back. ''*Delivery boy?*''

Elena looked as if she was digging her feet into the ground, but Logan kept pulling her anyway. ''So what's wrong with *delivery boy?*'' she said. ''Does it offend your country-club sensibilities, your highness?''

Logan sighed. ''You know Elena, the only snob around here is you.''

When Elena started to sputter, he looked back at Griffin. ''Bro?''

''Yeah?''

''What will you give me to get the pain-in-the-behind here out of your hair?''

Griffin's lips twitched and he seemed to relax a little, but his voice was wary. ''What do you have in mind?''

Logan looked down at the clearly silenced-by-outrage woman whose elbow he held, his gaze running over her from head to toe. ''A hundred bucks.''

''Done.''

Logan nodded back. ''Fine. C'mon Elena, I'll drive you home.''

Elena found her voice. ''A *hundred* dollars? You're asking your brother to pay a hun—''

''Shut up before I make it a thousand,'' Logan muttered, and walked her off into the darkness.

''Annie?'' Elena's voice warbled one last time through the night.

Annie stood on tiptoe to call over Griffin's shoulder. ''See you later, Elena.'' When she fell back to her heels she looked up at Griffin again. ''You never answered my question,'' she said.

As if he'd just realized his hands were still on her, Griffin quickly released her to shove them in his pockets. ''Answered…?''

''Why do you care where I was tonight?'' She took

a deep, brave breath. "For that matter, why are you *here* tonight?"

Griffin pulled his hands out of his pockets to run his fingers through his hair. Then he shoved them back in his pockets and rocked back on his heels. "Hell, Annie."

The weight of his gaze pressed against her skin like a palm, a hand, a needy mouth. *Annie suddenly realized he was looking at her the way she'd wanted him to look at her.* A shiver rolled down her back.

Precisely the way she'd wanted.

"Go ahead and say it. It's just you and me in the darkness, Griffin."

"I was worried about you," he said under his breath.

Annie sighed in disappointment. It always came down to that. The same old saw, the same old song. When was he going to get the idea she didn't *want* his concern? That she wanted *him.* How long would she have to wait?

Wait. The word sank into her consciousness. Why was she waiting again? Why shouldn't she just tell him, ask him, risk saying she wanted something more?

Risk getting what she truly desired?

Annie took a step forward. Griffin instantly edged back. She hesitated, unsure if she could really go through with this. But this was Griffin, she reminded herself. The daydream she'd been watching for years. The out-of-reach object of a crush from the big house. But he was also a real, flesh-and-blood man who right this instant was sending a euphoric zinging through her blood.

Ignoring the sudden, frantic beating of her heart, Annie took another step forward.

Though Griffin held his ground this time, even in the dim moonlight she could see his eyes narrow. "What is it? What's going on?"

She reached out and trailed her hand down the shirt covering his chest. It was soft, touchable silk. His gaze jumped from her to her hand, and *now* he took his own step. Back.

Annie licked her lips. "I've got to be honest with you—"

"I'm not sure I'm ready for that," Griffin hastily interjected.

She laughed softly. The wild bubbling in her blood was rushing faster now, but she wasn't afraid of the sensation. Instead, she felt all at once womanly and powerful with this big, usually commanding man shying away from her.

"Griffin," she said. "You've got to know I'm attracted to you."

He took another half-step back. "And you've got to know it's mutual." It sounded like he was gritting his teeth.

"I danced tonight," Annie said, smoothing her palms down her thighs. "Lots of men asked me."

"Yeah?" Griffin was definitely gritting his teeth.

"None of them make me feel like you do."

"And…how is that?" As if he couldn't help himself, Griffin reached out and tucked her hair behind her ear.

The touch streaked like fire down her neck, her breast. Half-shocked, half-excited by her own boldness, Annie caught his hand and pressed his palm to her breast. She closed her eyes and swayed into it.

He groaned. "Annie." His free hand came hard against the skin of her shoulder, bared by that rip, and jerked her against him. His other hand lightly squeezed her breast and then he kissed her, hard, too. Annie moaned, the hardness of hand, of mouth, contrasting with the light, almost delicate touch on her breast making heat swirl around her body. In her body.

Her thighs clenched against the ready, soft wetness just his kiss could create. Griffin lifted his head, but kept his hands on her, holding her against his hard chest, holding his palm gently against her breast. He sucked in a heavy, needy breath. "I can't resist you," he said.

"Why would you want to?" Annie whispered. She touched his lips with trembling fingers and he instantly opened them, to catch, lick, suck her fingers into his mouth.

Annie's blood hummed, her ears buzzed. His tongue swirled over her fingers one more time, but then he drew her hand from his mouth, baby-kissed the fingertips before he placed her hand at her side. Looking into her eyes, he stepped away. The last touch he relinquished was her breast, and now he dropped his gaze to watch his hand retreat from her body.

A long, deep breath shuddered into his chest. "I don't want to resist you," Griffin admitted. "But I should."

Annie curled her fingers into her palm, reveling in that sweet singing that still ran through her blood, in the knowledge that he desired her, too. "Tell me why you should resist, Griffin," she said quietly. "Explain that to me."

He lifted a hand. "You'll want more...expect..."

Annie caught his hand, squeezed it. *Now,* she thought. This is the moment to make up for all the chances never taken, all the risks avoided, all the times she'd hidden herself and watched through the windows instead of asking for what she wanted. Needed.

"The only thing I expect—" Annie started, but then had to haul in a quick breath to get it all out. "The only thing I expect is that you'll be good at this."

Better than me.

He hesitated. Tipping his head back, Griffin gazed up at the moon, as if looking for guidance. The moonlight caught in his eyes, and they glittered like silver. Then he looked at Annie, and with a quiet groan, pulled her back in his arms. "You make it hard to be noble."

She smiled tremulously. "I have it from a good source that nobility is highly overrated." Victory, desire and anticipation quivered inside her.

He groaned again and kissed her hard, then took her hand. "Annie, if you're sure, invite me in."

She was sure. So sure that words were hard to force past her tight throat. So, instead of talking, she mutely, hurriedly, led him up the steps to the cottage. She rushed to the door, and he rescued the key from her fumbling fingers to unlock and efficiently open it for her. But then he hung back, watching her.

Her heart pounding loud and insistent in her ears,

Annie grabbed his hand. No. He couldn't change his mind! Not now! She dragged him across the threshold and into her dark living room, backing quickly in the direction of the bedroom.

He laughed. "Wait, honey."

She shook her head and kept pulling. "No." Hadn't she been waiting too long already? What if he changed his mind? What if she lost her nerve?

He laughed again, a feathery, dark sound that ambled lazily down her spine like fingertips. "Let me at least shut the door."

Her fingers relaxed, and he leaned back to shove at the front door with one palm. It shut with a final *thud*.

Annie couldn't be happier. "Let's go. Hurry," she said hoarsely.

But Griffin stood firm. With another quiet laugh, he leaned back again and flipped a switch on the wall beside the front door. The lamp beside the love seat instantly lit the room with a dim glow.

Griffin tilted his head to one side, regarding her with a faint smile turning up the corner of his mouth. "This isn't a race, honey."

She detected the difference immediately. His earlier intensity was gone, replaced with a confident, smooth control. Trying to appear as nonchalant and composed as he was, she swallowed. "I—I know." Mercy. It was even difficult to talk with her pulse pounding so hard and so fast at her throat, at her wrists and even between her thighs.

He smiled again and ambled toward her. Annie took some more steps back, in the direction of the bedroom, hoping he would follow. The corner of his mouth kicked up again and he halted, looking around and sniffing appreciatively. "It smells good in here," he said. "Like chocolate and cinnamon."

Annie halted, too, though she thought she might scream. *It smells good in here?* Was it going to take all night to get him to the bedroom? Curling her hands into fists at her side, she tried to paste on her own little smile. Nonchalant. Composed.

"I baked earlier today," Annie explained. "Those are my Mexican Brownies you smell." Her hand shook as she brushed a piece of hair from her eyes. "Would you—would you like a taste of them? Or of something else?"

Argh. She wanted to shoot herself at the stupid, automatic offer. But heck, she was going to die anyway if he insisted on eating something before taking her to the bedroom.

Griffin smiled. "Oh, yeah," he said, "I want a taste." He crossed to her in two strides. "I want a taste of you."

His big hands framed her face and he leaned over to take her mouth.

Finally! Triumph blazed through her, then abruptly died as he lifted his head.

She was really going to scream. *"Griffin,"* came out instead. It was a needy, moany sound.

He smiled again, a big one this time that caused the corners of his blue eyes to tilt upward. "Yes, Annie?"

"You're torturing me," she confessed.

His smile became a full-fledged grin. "Good," he said. "You deserve it for every moment I've had to wonder about what you're going to remove next, or worse, what you've *already* removed.''

Her pantyless, braless day. A new kind of heat, embarrassed heat, ran up her neck. ''For your information,'' she said primly. ''I'm wearing everything I'm supposed to.''

Griffin laughed again and reached out to wrap her against his chest. ''Not for long.''

He looked down and tilted up her chin with his hand. ''Take me to your bedroom, Annie,'' he whispered. ''Take me to your bedroom and let me have my way with you.''

Yes. Oh, yes. Annie walked backward while he kissed her. It was a miraculous feat, because her head was spinning and she wasn't sure she was even touching ground as his mouth moved on hers and his tongue came inside.

Her fingers clutched his shoulders and she felt the strength in him, the maleness that should be frightening but was instead exciting. Annie slid her tongue against his and felt his muscles tense. That euphoric, thrilled zing in her blood changed, heating higher, speeding faster, into a steady, pulsing burn. Her desire leaped.

She needed more than his kiss. She needed his touch, his skin, she needed more *now*.

Something hit the back of Annie's thighs. The bed. He lifted his head, breaking the kiss, but she pulled his head back down, needing the contact, needing more kisses.

Griffin resisted. ''Slow down, sweetheart.''

''Don't wanna slow down.'' Even to her own ears,

her voice sounded giddy, high on desire. She went on tiptoe to press her mouth against his.

He groaned and let her kiss him, let her lick around the edges of his lips and then plunge her tongue into his mouth. Her heartbeat pounded in her chest, mighty knocks that made her whole body shudder. But when she pressed against him to let him feel what he did to her, Griffin stepped back.

She grabbed for him. "Don't go." The words jumped out.

"Oh, honey." Griffin's palm slid down the back of her head. "I'm not going anywhere. I couldn't. But we don't need to rush." The light on her bedside table flicked on. "I want to see you."

Annie jerked away from the light. It surprised her—frightened her, even—that he might be able to see her neediness on her face.

And then there was that insistent, unignorable pulse in her body. *Hurry hurry hurry.*

"I don't want the light," she said quickly.

"But I do." He flicked a teasing finger on her nose. "I want to see how pretty you are. I want to see everything I've been imagining since that day when I discovered you'd dumped all your underwear." His thumb brushed across her bottom lip.

Annie's breath caught in her throat. "Please, Griffin," she whispered.

He put his hands on her shoulders and ran his palms down her arms. Slowly. "Please, what, sweetheart?"

"Please, does it have to be so slow?"

He circled her waist and then smoothed his hands

up her ribs. His smile was slow, too. ''To please you, it does.''

Annie's eyes closed as his palms lightly covered her breasts. They immediately seemed to swell, to ache, and her teeth bit down on her lower lip to stop herself from crying out.

''Now don't do that,'' Griffin admonished. He leaned down to speak against her mouth. ''I'm afraid I'll have to insist that I get to do all the biting.'' He sucked in her lower lip and lightly scraped his teeth against it.

Annie shuddered, her nipples drawing into even tighter points. She leaned into his palms and his hands moved on her breasts, his fingers circling, touching, stroking, but never coming near the hard, aching centers.

Too slow, she thought, her mind hazy, but her blood pumping with insistent, needy desire. Touch me *there,* she commanded silently. But he kept up those almost-to-the-center touches, slow and gentle, and so good and yet not good enough at all.

It wasn't enough. Frustrated, Annie shifted her hands from his shoulders and moved to the front of his shirt. ''Annie,'' he whispered against her mouth, but she ignored him as she worked on the buttons, unfastening four. With trembling hands, she spread the sides of his shirt and touched her fingers to his chest.

He groaned, breaking their kiss.

The sound was good, but better was the heated skin of his chest, the hard muscles and the crisp hair she could see glinting like gold in the lamplight. Annie placed her palms over Griffin's heartbeat, thrilled at how heavily it thundered against them. Then she slid her hands outward.

When the edge of her palms brushed the hard points of his nipples, he caught his breath, stepped back. His shirt whipped over his head.

It was the quickest movement he'd made. Annie's pulse kicked up another impossible notch and she reached for him.

He grabbed her hands, keeping all that golden skin and all those hard muscles out of her range. With a commanding touch, he placed her hands at her sides, then reached for the hem of her top. "Yours now, too," he whispered.

Her skin goosebumped as he drew the fabric over her ribcage, over her breasts, over her head. Then he tossed it to the floor and stared at what he'd revealed. Beneath her pale pink, translucent bra, Annie's breasts rose swollen and aching. Her nipples pressed against the fabric, ruched and darker than she'd ever seen them.

Annie reached for Griffin to bring him close, but he caught her hands again and once more set them at her sides. "Always in such a hurry," he said. "I'm going to have to teach you patience."

Patience! Annie thought she'd suffocate from it as he touched her breasts again, his forefingers drawing circles over her bra, large circles that turned smaller, and then small circles that turned larger so that once again he never touched her nipples.

Despite his earlier order, she bit her bottom lip to try to keep control. Griffin didn't seem to notice, not when his focus was so calm, so single-minded as he shifted one hand to toy with the front clasp of her bra.

Annie's entire body tensed, every nerve begging for him to touch her skin, unleash her from the waiting.

His fingers tightened on the clasp. Annie held her breath.

With an expert twist, the catch was released. The fabric of the bra sprang away from her straining breasts to catch on her hard, distended nipples. Annie moaned, then Griffin brushed the fabric free as he bent his head to touch her with his mouth.

Annie's body jerked. He touched her nipple with his tongue, painted it gently with the wet tip, and Annie's lower body clenched, going softer, hotter, even more ready for him. There was an ache inside now, too, an emptiness she'd never before knew needed filling.

But she couldn't think how to tell him about it, how to tell him to hurry to do something about it, as he slowly, strongly, sucked her nipple into his mouth. Sensation waved through her, heat and desire. She clasped his head between her hands.

He moved, but she didn't have time to protest, because a heavy breath later he was sitting on the bed and had pulled her between his thighs. His mouth was on her other breast and he painted that nipple, too, with gentle, painstaking licks that heightened the sensation in her breast, setting every nerve ending twitching with anticipation.

She moaned. "Griffin, please. Hurry."

His eyelashes lifted, and he looked at her, as if to judge her neediness. Then he gave in, tugging on her nipple with a soft bite before sucking on it, soft and gentle, hard and strong. Desire melted her strength, and as Annie's knees gave out, Griffin slid backward on the bed, taking her with him.

Her breasts pressed against his chest, the nipples he'd wet with his mouth against his own hot skin. "Mm," he said, looking into her eyes and stroking her cheeks with his thumbs. "You taste good."

Annie couldn't believe he could still look so lazy and light and in control. She wanted more, she wanted it all, she wanted it *now*.

"No more slow," she said urgently. She pressed against him, pushing her pelvis into his, seeking the sensations her body was clamoring for. "I don't like slow."

His hands clamped on her hips, holding her still. "*I* like slow."

Even to her passion-hazed mind, Annie realized that what he liked was control. That what he liked was control of himself.

"Don't tease me," she said. Her desire was so hot, her need burning in her nipples, her breasts, between her legs. "Please, Griffin. I don't want to wait anymore."

She'd been waiting for this moment her entire life.

His expression softened. "Oh, honey. I'm not trying to make you wait. Don't you know? I want you to anticipate."

Her mouth turned down. "I've anticipated enough already." She didn't let his sudden, small grin detract her. "Please." Though he was trying to hold her hips still, she circled them against his hardness.

His eyes closed and he sucked in a breath. "Do that again," he said.

She pushed against him, that empty, aching part of

her finding the long ridge of his arousal. It felt so good against her, male and hard and the very thing she needed to ease the empty throbbing inside her.

Griffin tugged on the elastic waistband of her long skirt, and he pushed it down, his palms brushing against the silky fabric of her panties. Annie's heart started thundering again, and without thinking she kicked the rest of the skirt away.

He clamped his hands over her hips once more. Two of his fingers slid below the top band of her bikini panties. "Do it again, honey, move."

Annie pressed against him once more, but now free of the constricting fabric of her skirt, her thighs slid over Griffin's hips to bracket them. When she pressed down, he pressed up, and his erection pushed into the soft heat of her center.

Annie shuddered. *"Griffin."*

"Shh." He soothed his palms over her hips and down her bottom, but she realized his hands were inside her panties and now he pushed those down, too. Annie had to bring her legs together to kick them away, and when she did, Griffin rolled from underneath her to shuck his shoes, jeans and briefs.

He tossed off his shirt, then stopped to deal with the foil packet he must have had with him. Eyes widening, Annie watched as he matter-of-factly unrolled a condom to cover his erection.

She swallowed. It was very big. She had no idea how it was going to fit.

Panic slightly dulled the edge of her desire.

"Annie?" Griffin pulled her against him as before, yet now she could feel every inch of his heated skin. She stretched her legs against his, the tickly abrasion of the hair on his just enough to make her shudder again. Delicious.

He ran his hands down her naked back to cup her bottom in his big palms. "Do it again, Annie."

Helplessly, she obeyed. As she pressed down against him, he pulled her thighs over his hips. That heavy, hard part of him—it—moved against her folds. He moved smoothly over them, the path slickened by all their play.

He stroked against her again and pleasure streaked through her. A demanding pleasure that reminded her of that aching, empty place he was so close to.

The place it belonged.

"Griffin—"

"We're not going to hurry this either," he said.

That hadn't been what she was going to say. As a matter of fact, the more she thought about the size of him—it—the more she thought she'd better tell him—

Her mind blanked when he rolled her over and took her breast in his mouth.

Needy desire washed over her again, made her roll up her hips, made her arch when he explored the slick folds with one of his long fingers. That empty place inside her burned, burned by the new intrusion when he explored her with two fingers, burned with the need for something to happen, for something to happen there.

Right there.

Right now.

"Griffin," she said urgently. Oh, please, he couldn't make her wait now. Because there was a rhythm he had begun with his fingers. It twisted the tension in her body. She felt her muscles straining, her heart pounding, her breath coming in great rasps.

She closed her eyes, but even then she could still see him, his darkly golden head against her breast, his big hand between her splayed thighs. It was erotic and exciting and everything she'd ever wanted. Heat streaked from hip to hip, banding her body, a band that tightened to excruciating pleasure with every tug of his mouth, with every firm thrust of his fingers. The sensations came together, gathering force, then more force.

Annie's breath caught. Her back arched. The band of heat broke. Bliss shook her body.

Chapter Nine

Griffin watched Annie climax, holding himself under strict control. Seeing her lost to passion was satisfying. Gratifying. But every pulsing clutch of her inner muscles on his invading fingers spiked his lust to new, dangerous heights.

He wanted to bury himself inside her. He wanted to consume her with a hunger that was as startling as it was hard to keep leashed.

His gaze focused on her, he saw Annie's body slowly stop trembling and her eyelashes lift. The giddiness of sated desire glittered in them. "Griffin," she whispered, reaching for him.

Instantly, the urge to crawl up her body and thrust inside her flamed up his spine. He resisted, telling himself to master the need, not to let it master him.

Soft and slow was his M.O., the way he liked it,

the way he knew was good for the woman in his arms. But something about Annie, her sweet body, her sweet taste, something about *her* made him want to push and possess and lust and lunge.

She was messing with his head and, damn it, he liked control of that, too.

"Griffin," Annie whispered again, her hands on his shoulders.

"I'm here, sweetheart," his voice was hoarse, but he didn't think she could detect what it was costing him to stay calm. Clamping down on his driving need, he kissed each one of her nipples once more and slid up her body to take her mouth.

She welcomed him, her lips so soft and easy that he focused on that, on *soft and easy,* as he knelt between her legs. He fitted himself to the notch of her body, gritting his teeth as his shaft first touched her searing heat.

Slow and easy and in control.

He moved his hips forward gently, knowing how tight she was, knowing that even after her climax it wouldn't be easy for her to take him. "Relax, baby," he whispered against her ear, but the words were for himself, too, to keep himself from letting go and plunging into her.

She made a small sound and he stopped moving, letting her get accustomed to the feel of just that small amount of him inside her. Her breath was coming in little pants, and he kissed her cheek, her mouth, then palmed her breast.

Annie arched into his touch.

That sweet berried nipple rising to meet his hand nearly did him in. *Slow and easy!* he reminded himself, just barely holding onto his sanity as he pushed forward the slightest bit more.

Damn, she was tight. His body shuddered against the agonizingly good sensation, but he knew there was something more than sensation eating at his control. It was Annie, the scent of her, the taste of her. He touched the plump, soft flesh of her breast again, and Annie arched higher. His thumb brushed her nipple and she made a needy sound that echoed in his head, his blood.

When he brushed it once more, when he felt it pucker incredibly tighter against the pad of his thumb, the needy sound was his. The need was his. Desire and lust pounded in him.

He canted his hips, thinking to ease back, thinking to cool himself down, but then Annie lifted her mouth. She joined it with his, her heated sweetness so good, so damn good. The last of Griffin's control flew out of reach as he thrust his tongue into Annie's mouth and his throbbing arousal between Annie's open thighs.

Wild pleasure seared him.

And then her cry registered in his brain. And the new tension in her body.

His eyes snapped open. He looked at her, at the startled, near-pained expression on her face. "Annie?"

She swallowed. "Surprise?"

"Oh, Annie." He was pulsing inside her body, no less hungry for her, but now aware he was the first man ever to *be* inside her body. "Why didn't you say something?"

"Sh." She put her fingers over his mouth. "Why

don't you stop talking? I'm pretty sure there's more to it than this.''

He kissed her fingers, groaning again. Sliding his hands to her hips, he tilted them, and pressed forward a little more. ''Relax, baby,'' he said. ''Let me show you how it goes.''

He could do this, he thought, almost-relief cooling his blood. Annie's virginity was the perfect antidote to his raging lust. Slow and easy was the only way to do this, was the only way to show her how it could be between them.

Wanting to cause her the least amount of discomfort, he stayed deep inside her, just flexing his hips to let her get used to the fullness of his body joined with hers. He kissed her, deeply, with rhythmic thrusts of his tongue so that she'd understand the cadence of arousal. Then he reached between them to touch her just above where their bodies joined. He found the small swollen knot that he plied gently and stroked mercilessly so that she would know pleasure was due her, was hers.

When she climaxed the second time with his fingers on her and his body inside hers, he thought he'd watch that, too. But as her skin flushed and her nipples turned even rosier, Griffin closed his eyes.

Heat was pumping through his body, pleasure teetering on the brink, and it was Annie, her inner muscles tightening even more, who pushed him forward. Over.

Without any more movement, with only the sensation of Annie wrapped around him, contracting around him, he fell deep, deeper, as, from far away, he heard himself call out her name.

* * *

Griffin stared at Annie's bedroom ceiling, the moonlight shining through her window shifting leaf shadows against the plaster. Her head was pillowed on his shoulder, her silky cheek against his chest, her hand rested limply just above his navel. When she exhaled, her breaths even and calm, his chest hair stirred.

He envied her serenity. Hell, he'd settle for just one-eighth of his own usual post-coital calm. That was what he was good at, the slow and easy sex followed by the friendly, wasn't-that-fun? afterglow.

But damn, it was different this time. Instead of his usual aplomb, his blood continued to pulse heavily and if Annie moved her fingers just a couple of inches south, she'd discover his body was still half hard, not even close to being sated. He hadn't had enough of her.

She'd been a virgin. The thought jabbed over and over like a throbbing headache against his brain. God. He'd appointed himself her protector, but that had been like setting the wolf to watch over the lamb. An innocent, take-his-breath-away, tasty lamb.

What the hell had he done?

Annie moved, turning onto her belly to look into his face. "Don't go all regretful on me," she said softly.

He closed his eyes. "Why didn't you tell me?" he asked, his voice hoarse.

She didn't pretend not to know what he meant. "Because it wasn't that important to me."

He groaned at the blatant lie. "Please. You're almost twenty-five years old and you're a virgin. Now you're trying to tell me it's not that important to you?''

''*Was* a virgin,'' she said calmly.

He gritted his teeth. ''That's right. You *were* a virgin. Now explain yourself.''

''I don't have to.''

That headache started jabbing at his brain again. ''Don't play games with me, Annie.''

''My choices, my past are my own business, wouldn't you agree? You'll notice I didn't ask you for a history report before I asked you to bed.''

''Because you spied on most of my history,'' he muttered.

She laughed. ''Not all of it, I'm sure.''

Griffin didn't know what to say to that. He didn't know what to say to *her*. But it seemed incredibly obvious that going to bed with a virgin was a lot different from going to bed with a more experienced woman. Or maybe the real difference was that the woman he'd gone to bed with was Annie.

His head hurt again.

Annie, damn it.

Annie.

He ran a finger down her warm cheek and across her small, pointed chin, and she leaned into his touch. She was such a little cat. ''Are you okay?'' he asked. ''I didn't hurt you?''

''Mm.'' She rolled over and he shifted so that their shoulders touched and their heads shared a pillow. ''It was nice,'' Annie said. ''And I'm fine, thank you.''

''Nice? Just…nice?''

''Is that the wrong thing to say?''

He tried to ignore the small rush of annoyance and

keep the conversation light. "A superlative or two wouldn't be out of order."

Her shoulders moved in a silent laugh. "I'm sorry."

"That's the trouble with virgins." Griffin shook his head, his voice sad. His tension eased as he let himself fall into a more casual, less personal after-sex patter. "You have to teach them *everything*. Superlatives are a definite yes. Say stupendous, sweetheart."

Her shoulders shook again. "Stupendous sweetheart," she parroted.

"No sass," he said sternly. "Say stupendous."

"Stupendous." He ignored her bubble of laughter.

"Incredible," he prompted next.

She swallowed the laugh this time and her obedient "incredible" came out part-hiccup.

"Good." He paused. "Now say enormous."

She went silent, and he thought maybe he'd finally shocked her. But then the word came out, just a little strained. "Enormous…"

He was nodding with satisfaction when she added, "…ego."

Then she laughed. At him, with him, it didn't matter, because the sound of her helpless, tickled laughter told him everything was going to be all right. Or so he thought, until the laughter was joined by tears that glittered silver in the moonlight and ran down Annie's cheeks. His breath disappeared and he couldn't help himself from reaching out to catch one of those fateful drops on his fingertip.

Her watery laughter abruptly died. "Oh, Griffin," she said.

"Oh, Annie." *Damn it, Annie.*

"I'm not what you had in mind, am I?"

No, Griffin thought. Not at all. He'd come back to Strawberry Bay to return to old routines, old patterns. He'd assumed he'd focus on work and take a little time off here and there for a casual sexual relationship.

One phone call and one visit to the police station may have altered his plans a bit, but he'd committed himself to taking care of Annie then, not taking her to bed. "I don't know what to do with you," he said honestly.

"Why do you think you have to do something with me?"

He ignored the irritation in her voice. "Annie, our families have a long association." Logan, his mother, her mother, his father even, would kill him if he hurt Annie.

She scooted away from him. "That's right. I'm the housekeeper's daughter."

"Don't be stupid, Annie."

"Maybe I think *you're* the one that's stupid. This was *my* choice, Griffin. You didn't 'do something' to me in this bed. I don't need you to 'do something' with me now."

He didn't like her attitude. It was too casual. Maybe not casual enough. Who the hell knew?

Anger starting to burn in his gut, Griffin sat up, stuffing the pillow behind his back. "Damn it, Annie, I knew it. It's happening already."

She sat up, too, holding the sheet against her breasts. "Happening already?"

"I thought we had a pleasant friendship going. But now I can see the sex has complicated that."

"Pleasant friendship?"

An odd buzzing started in his ears. "Stop quoting me back to me."

"Maybe I'm hoping that what you say will sound as ridiculous to you as it does to me."

Ridiculous. What was ridiculous was how pissed off he was starting to feel. This isn't what he did in bed. In bed, after sex, he was the gentleman, the light and entertaining lover. Women he'd just brought to orgasm—twice—didn't make him angry. Sex didn't leave him feeling like he wanted more.

This was all Annie's fault. "Annie—"

"Don't say it," she said.

He tried clamping down on his steadily rising temper as he swung around on the mattress. "Don't say what?" With an angry swipe, he grabbed his jeans off the floor and stepped into them. "You have no idea what I'm going to say, just like you have no idea the trouble our having sex is going to cause me." He closed his eyes at the clumsy gaffe. "You. Us."

She was silent as he stood. He wasn't going to look at her face. He wasn't even going to bother rooting around for his shoes or shirt.

"You think this was a mistake," Annie said.

A huge mistake. Stupendous. Incredible. Enormous. And he was that big a jerk, too, because he muttered, loud enough for her to hear, "Give the lady an A."

So to punish himself, he stalked back to the house in the cold, his bare feet smarting under the sting of the inch-thick pea-gravel on the path through the oaks. When he passed the gazebo, he kept his head down. Looking at it would remind him too much of Annie.

It would remind him of all that he'd missed seeing in her those many years ago. Of all that he'd miss about her now.

Early the next morning, Annie slipped into the ten-car Chase garage and dumped Griffin's shoes, shirt and boxers on the hood of his Mercedes. Then she narrowed her eyes, and visualizing one of the car tires as his backside, she gave it a good, swift kick. Griffin apparently wanted her to hate him, and Annie figured she just might do him that favor.

Except she was honest enough with herself to realize that he was as mad at himself as she was. Anyway, the situation was partly her fault.

Oh, fine. All her fault.

Maybe she hadn't known how making love with Griffin would be—her heart stuttered just remembering his hands on her skin, his body joining with hers—but she'd known Griffin. His protective instincts had kicked into high gear when he'd realized she'd been a virgin.

He thought he had to protect her from himself.

Annie had watched enough women waltz in and out of his life to know he wasn't seeking commitment or complications. It shouldn't surprise her that he'd view Annie Smith, the girl next door, the virginal housekeeper's daughter, as someone who wanted one and promised the other.

Sure, there was that intriguing and almost incomprehensible case of him actually on the brink of a marriage proposal once upon a time, but Annie was halfway to thinking he'd made up the story.

Griffin didn't want a woman permanently in his life. Sitting in the bank parking lot two days ago, she'd accepted that and decided she'd take what time she could get.

If it wasn't enough, she had only herself to blame.

Without knowing what else to do, Annie reentered her cottage and decided to give a stab at cooking her blue mood away. She turned up the stereo and turned on the oven and tried losing herself in making the pastry shells she would fill with a seafood bisque for Mrs. Worthington's bridge party on Monday. With the delicate golden-brown shells cooling on a rack, Annie moved straight into preparing the buttery press cookies she planned to serve with a strawberry sorbet as dessert.

The planning of menus and cooking of dishes usually fulfilled both her creative and nurturing urges. Long ago, she'd discovered that the smells of baking wrapped her in a homey comfort that eased the undercurrent of loneliness in her life. For a woman with only half a family, spending most of her days in the kitchen went partway to filling the hole in her heart. But today, her bleak mood wasn't lifting.

Finally, the only thing left to prepare the next morning was the bisque itself and an arugula and radicchio salad. With a lemon vinaigrette whipped together and sitting in her refrigerator, Annie could no longer avoid remembering the night before.

To get away from the shiver-inducing memories and thoughts of the man who was the source of them, she jumped into her little car and headed toward town.

Annie wasn't surprised to find herself at the door of her mother's apartment. Once inside, she breathed out a sigh as she flopped onto the familiar, comfy couch. "This is good," she said, smiling at her mom. Annie ran her palms over the nubby fabric, the blue-and-white pattern as familiar as the smile lines around her mother's eyes. "Some days I wouldn't mind being ten years old again, when my biggest problem was whether or not I'd finish my homework packet by Friday."

"And you wouldn't have had to worry about that if you'd spent more time with the packet and less time stalking Griffin."

Annie winced. Great, the subject she was here to avoid, not that she wanted to let her mother in on that. "I never stalked him." Annie bit her bottom lip. "Exactly."

Her mother just smiled. "Exactly."

Searching quickly for another topic, Annie's gaze snagged on a new postcard lying on the end table. "Another of Aunt Jen's persuasion pieces?" Annie asked, reaching for it. This one pictured a roly-poly panda cub from the San Diego Zoo. She flipped it over, her eyes widening at what her aunt had written in her distinctive, loopy cursive.

"Hey, Mom. Aunt Jen says she has a man for you?" Annie grinned in her mother's direction. "Someone from her book group?"

Her mother grimaced. "Your Aunt Jen is a big tease."

Annie wiggled her eyebrows. "You've got to go there and meet him, Mom. Check out whether you want to finally surrender to Aunt Jen's enticements and move.''

''I couldn't move.''

Her mother's tone wasn't unpleasant, but it was final. Annie frowned as her mother got up and moved toward the window, minutely adjusting the family photos arranged on the table nearby.

Silently Annie watched her mom brush her finger across the photo of Annie's father. Then again. Annie frowned deeper. It wasn't as if there was anything marring the frame or the glass. In Natalie Smith's house dust didn't dare adhere to surfaces. ''Mom...''

''You should open the door, Annie.''

''Huh?'' Annie asked absently, trying to put words to her uneasiness.

''Elena's here.''

Proof to the words, a no-nonsense fist battered at the door. Annie headed toward it, half relieved and half dismayed at the interruption. Something about her mother was uneasily tickling her mind.

As Annie opened the door, Elena blew whatever it was right out of Annie's head. ''Oh my God!'' Elena's eyes were round. ''Don't lie to me. I can see the truth on your face. You've gone ahead and done it. You've gone ahead and...''

Annie glared and Elena's mouth snapped shut. Then a sticky smile turned up Elena's lips and her gaze traveled over Annie's shoulder to her mother. ''...you've gone ahead and done something new with your hair.''

Rolling her eyes, Annie grabbed her friend by the elbow and pulled her inside. ''Fancy meeting you here,'' she said through her teeth.

"I've been trying to get you all day. Once I got tired of talking to your machine I went to the grocery store and then drove by here on the off chance that I might find you and then find out—"

"That new thing I've done with my hair?" Annie interjected.

Elena's eyes swiveled toward Natalie Smith, swiveled back toward Annie. "Yeah, yeah. Your hair."

Natalie laughed and both Annie and Elena jumped guiltily. "Why don't I go in the kitchen and whip up some tea and cookies? You two can talk more privately then."

Annie winced. "Thanks, Mom."

Elena grinned. "You're still the coolest, Natalie." When Annie's mother disappeared, Elena shook her head, her smile dying. "She makes me wish my mom was still alive," she said wistfully.

Annie touched her friend's arm. "I know."

Elena straightened her shoulders. "For Gabby's sake, of course. *I'm* fine. I don't need anyone."

Gabby was Elena's teenage sister, Gabriella. "I know you're fine. Gabby is, too. You're doing a great job raising her."

"Of course." Elena's spine went that much straighter.

Annie gazed at her friend with true affection. Never betray a weakness was Elena's motto. And she could hold a grudge for a hundred years, but it was only because she was so afraid of being hurt. Speaking of which...

"So did you and Logan make it home okay last night?"

But Elena wouldn't be distracted. "Forget that

man.'' With a cavalier wave of her hand, she eliminated him from possible discussion. ''Tell me about Griffin. What, how, when, and most particularly, why?''

Annie blinked. ''Why?'' Elena wanted to know *why?*

Elena's eyebrows raised. ''Don't bother denying anything. The outcome of last night was a given once I saw the way Griffin was looking at you. So…was he there for breakfast this morning?''

Annie's cheeks burned. ''No.''

''Then why is a fair question. You had to know he wasn't going to fall easily.''

Annie shook her head. ''I went in with my eyes open. I never thought he was going to fall at all.''

''Please!'' Elena threw herself onto the couch. ''This is your best friend you're talking to. The one who you let read every entry in your diary.''

''From when I was seventeen.''

''So? Some things don't change. What exactly happened?''

Annie sat primly on the rocker beside the couch. ''I'm certainly not going to talk about it. I'm not going to kiss and tell.''

Elena frowned. ''No?'' She rubbed her palms on her jeans obviously thinking, then sat forward. ''Tell me about Fannie, then.''

''Fannie?'' Annie blinked.

''Yeah. Fannie. See, you can tell me a little story about what happened to Fannie and then you're not really revealing any private, between-a-man-and-a-woman secrets.''

Annie's jaw dropped. "How much coffee did you have this morning?"

"Do you want a different name? Yannie? That works. Yannie and...Stiffin."

"I'm not going to call him Stiffin!"

"Mm." Elena grimaced. "I can see your point. Yannie and Biffin, then."

"Elena." Annie spoke slowly and clearly, hoping her words would penetrate her friend's not normally thick head. "I'm not calling myself Yannie. Griffin is not Biffin. I think you've lost your mind."

Elena fell back against the couch cushions. "I'm worried that you'll lose your heart," she said seriously.

Not for the first time, Annie wished she knew what past romantic tragedy—tragedies?—had hardened Elena. "I didn't go into it expecting *anything,* Elena, so there's no way I can get hurt, okay?"

That *was* the truth, right? Annie had no right to be hurt, nor any right to expect more than what Griffin had given her last night. Well, it would have been nice to have him around for breakfast, but that was a silly point.

Just as all her old daydreams and childish diary entries had been merely silly fantasies. Silly Cinderella stuff. She'd chalk the whole thing up to experience.

Chapter Ten

Monday afternoon, with the check for Mrs. Worthington's catering job in hand and the disquieting memory of the armed robbery still bubbling way too near the top of her consciousness, Annie's first thought was that enough was enough.

Well, no. That was her second thought. Her first thought—of Griffin's moon-gilded body lifting over hers—had taken her cruising by the corporate headquarters of Chase Electronics in the northwestern section of Strawberry Bay. She assumed Griffin's office would be one with a dynamite ocean view somewhere in the six floors of the green glass-and-steel building that bordered Chase Boulevard, though several other company buildings sprawled around the main one.

She didn't catch a glimpse of him, however, even though she craned her neck to check out the parking lot for a sign of his platinum-colored convertible. When that neck-craning nearly caused her to slam into the car in front of her, Annie forced herself to admit that driving by a man's place of work—a man who dumped you after one fabulous session in bed, no less—was pitiful. Worse yet, juvenile.

That's when she'd met her eyes in the rearview mirror and given herself a lecture.

"First, you need to forget about him."

Yes.

"Next, you need to get over the bank robbery."

That's right.

"You need to take what happened and let it empower you, not victimize you."

Absolutely right.

She looked at the fat check sitting on the passenger seat of her catering van and bit her bottom lip. "You need to go into the bank."

No way.

Annie swallowed, willing to cut herself a compromise. "Not *that* branch. But how about the one on Chase and Seventh? Walk inside, make your deposit, walk out. Then you'll have proven something to me."

Like what?

Annie didn't know her inner voice could sound so suspicious. "That you're strong. That a little thing like a bank robber or the wrong man in bed can't keep you down."

The wrong *man in bed?*

"Oh, shush. Just remember we're forgetting about him. That's the most important part," Annie said firmly. With a determined twist of her steering wheel, she guided the van into the Savings and Loan's parking lot. "He's nothing to us."

Except Mr. Nothing is pretty good at making us talk to ourselves.

Annie jumped out of her seat and slammed the door behind her. "Shut up," she said crossly.

"Pardon me?" An elderly gentleman unlocking the door of the car in the space beside Annie's gave her a strange look.

The embarrassment was enough to get her dashing for the lobby doors. They closed behind her with a click, and Annie froze, giving her physical and mental state a brief once-over. Heartbeat steady. Legs ready to function. Anxiety at a definitely manageable level. Pleased, she stepped up to one of the nearby elbow-high desks and prepared to endorse her check for deposit.

A soft voice intruded. "Annie. Uh. Hi."

The hairs on the back of her neck leaped. Startled, Annie whipped around. "Joey," she managed to choke out. Her heartbeat drummed, a primal predator-in-the-offing warning, even though her logical mind registered nothing more threatening than her cohort in shyness, her partner in paste and scissors, Joey Delvecchio.

She swallowed. "Good…good to see you, Joey." Her gaze focused on the diamond pattern of his expensive-looking tie then followed it down to the snazzy, shiny black loafers on his feet. "You look nice."

"I'm surprised to see you here." Joey's mouth stretched in a smile.

Annie blinked, hypnotized for a minute by what

looked like new pearly whites. Joey had capped his teeth. Amazing what selling a few Yugos could do for a guy. ''I have something to deposit.'' She waved the check which was starting to look a little damp around the edges, thanks to her suddenly sweaty palms. ''You?''

''I have business here, too.''

Nodding, Annie tried thinking calming thoughts to control her still wildly thrumming heart. Sailboats. Blue skies. Crème brûlée. But the panic that had blind-sided her refused to subside, even with the familiar Joey Delvecchio just inches away.

Sucking in a deep breath, Annie looked down and fumbled awkwardly inside her purse for a pen. ''Well, it was good seeing you again, Joey.''

''Let me help you.''

Joey reached out and Annie inexplicably found herself jerking away. Her turning shoulder whacked the chest of a man who had just walked up behind her. He grunted, she gasped, her purse, her check, her just-found pen fell to the floor.

''I'm sorry!'' Annie's gaze jumped from the spill on the linoleum to the man she'd just de-aired.

He—Griffin—looked at her with a rueful smile. ''I think that's my line.''

Annie's heartbeat kicked up again. At this rate she'd have to stop by the cardiac care unit on her way home for a pacemaker. But her anxiety eased even as his fingers brushed a lock of hair behind her ear.

His eyes narrowed. ''Something's wrong,'' he said.

Before she could answer, Joey pushed the things he'd stooped to retrieve from the floor into her hands. Anxiety bubbled again, but Annie controlled it this time, taking in another long breath. "Thanks, Joey." She looked between the two men. "Do you know Griffin? Joey Delvecchio, this is Griffin Chase. Griffin, Joey."

The two men shook hands, Joey wearing a smile that wasn't any less diffident for all the gleaming teeth behind it. "I guess I'll be going now, Annie," he said.

"Okay. Bye, Joey." Annie frowned, wondering if she should point out he'd never actually gone up to a teller. "I'll see you at the dealership."

Griffin gave the other man a chilly nod before Joey left the bank. Then he turned on Annie with a frown. "I don't like the way he looks at you."

Annie ignored Griffin and took another self-inventory. Whew. Heartbeat? Nearly normal. Respiration? She was managing that pretty well, too, in and out, in and out. With the physical stuff back under control, that meant she had energy for the emotional.

Which was easy. Seeing to her emotional needs meant ignoring Griffin. Turning her back on him, she slapped her check on the plastic, wood-embossed desk and started to sign her name.

"What happened before I came in?" he asked. "You looked upset."

She knew her account number by heart, so she filled that in, too, and then headed for the teller line.

Griffin trailed her. "Stop pretending I'm not here," he said, obviously irritated.

Impossible, with his delicious, expensive scent trailing her, too. She shot him a look. "Why *are* you here?"

He was wearing a dark blue suit and Annie wondered if he'd had it hand-tailored. It followed the line of his broad shoulders and lean frame that perfectly.

Without meeting her eyes, he shoved his hands in his pockets. "I saw your van as I drove back to the office from a meeting across town."

She raised her eyebrows.

His hands dug deeper in his pockets and his jaw set.

She let her eyebrows rise another inch.

He narrowed his gaze and answered the unspoken question. "I was worried about you, damn it."

"I'm fine." She turned away from him as the line moved forward. And she *was* fine, she realized. Now that she'd made it through that momentary panic attack, there was no real residual fear, no big bad memories pressing down on her. When her turn came for the teller, she walked confidently up to the window and took care of business.

When she turned back around, Griffin was still in the lobby, looking just as half irritated and half surly as before. Annie, on the other hand, felt like a new woman. She'd done it. She'd overcome her banking cowardice!

She'd walked up to the teller, no problem. She'd walk over Griffin with the same nonchalance.

Humming, Annie pushed through the bank doors and into the spring sunshine. He dogged her footsteps, but she pretended he wasn't there. No. Nope. She wasn't going to let him get to her, not his delicious scent, not his melt-her-heart good looks, not his lousy mood.

All the way to the car, all the way through unlocking her car, she kept up her tuneless hum. He smoldered behind her, but she didn't let even a hint of his heat affect her cool composure.

Until he opened his mouth. "You can't still be mad at me," he said.

Annie tried, she really did. She reminded herself that she'd decided to chalk up their lovemaking to experience and that she'd gone into this with her eyes open, not expecting anything. She tried thinking about the sky and sailboats again, and then bypassed thoughts of crème brûlée for the even more bland tapioca pudding.

But her grip on the doorhandle of the van was white-knuckled and she knew her own voice was tight. "Of course I'm not mad at you."

"Liar."

Well, duh.

"Turn around and look at me, Annie."

To prove to him how easy that was, how easy it had been to gain and lose her first lover in the space of one night, Annie turned. Crossing her arms over her chest, she leaned casually against the warm side of the van.

"There's not one reason for you to be angry at me."

"Right." She even smiled a little at him.

"I did us both a favor."

"Yep," she said. *Nope,* she thought. "You're right again."

"Damn it, Annie. I *am* right. We want different things."

Wanting different things. Wrong. Untrue. "Uh-huh." Annie agreed though, then narrowed her gaze. Was she imagining things or was his face turning red?

"We do," he insisted, as if she'd disagreed. His face was definitely red.

"Right," she said again. There was great satisfaction in needling him. "I want to live in Strawberry Bay, the place you just came back to."

He stared.

"I want to make a success of my company." She shrugged. "You seem pretty intent on doing the same with Chase Electronics."

He made a noise deep in his throat.

Annie was starting to like the upper hand. She was starting to feel really good and powerful about throwing his "we want different things" back in his face. "I like to cook, you like to eat. I like to laugh and to talk and I've had a fabulous time doing both with you."

Confidence was zinging through her blood. The timid little girl who'd hero-worshiped Griffin from afar had definitely taken a hike, for good. Let him see what he could have had, Annie thought. Let him weep at the one who had gotten away. She was never going to let him close enough to hurt her again.

"So, I see what you mean." Annie smiled again. "You're absolutely, completely, one-hundred-percent right." *Hah.*

"About the most important things, I am," he said quietly.

Annie's confidence dropped from sixty to zero in 2.2 seconds. She swallowed as he stepped closer.

"Don't try to pretend you're something you're not," Griffin said.

She swallowed again. "What do you mean by that?"

"Orange blossoms. Anniversary bands. You're looking forward to years of connubial bliss."

Commitment, Annie thought. "Eventually I hope for that," she said carefully. The fantasy that her "eventually" would be none other than Griffin was a childish one, of course. Put away long ago.

"Well, you won't get that from me. I told you. I've accepted I'm not the marrying kind." Griffin's face was completely blank, though his blue eyes glittered. "Believe me, Annie."

She tried holding them back, she really did, but her hurt feelings broke free from all her cool nonchalance, anyway. "Of course I know that's not you, Griffin. I'm not a believer in fairy tales, even though you did make me feel a bit like Cinderella for a little while that night."

He reached out a hand as if he was going to touch her face and she brushed it away. "Don't," she said. Those were *not* tears burning the back of her eyes. "Don't touch me." So much for not letting him see he'd affected her.

"Annie." His voice was hoarse and he pushed the hand she'd batted away through his hair. "I just know I can't do commitment."

"I wasn't asking for a lifetime, Griffin." She couldn't stop the words any more than she could stop breathing. "But to be honest I did think I might get more than a single night—no, that wasn't even a whole night, was it?"

He winced. "Annie—"

"Don't worry about it. Gee, if you'd stayed until morning I might have considered our encounter a one-night stand. This way I can tell myself that it was only that the clock struck midnight and the pumpkin arrived.''

She got into the van before he could stop her. He banged on the window and was mouthing something, but she ignored him and put the vehicle into reverse.

Then she drove away, all the while wishing she could reverse the entire situation with Griffin just as easily.

It was turning dark as Annie curled up on her love seat with a cup of tea and a stack of her latest cooking magazines. With less than three weeks before Mr. and Mrs. Chase's fortieth anniversary, Annie needed inspiration. For the party, she wanted to create something special using the asparagus which would soon come into season.

She looked over the glossy, colorful photographs, waiting for one to trigger her imagination. That ability to invent had been her best friend during her lonely childhood. The summer Griffin had stayed with some relatives in Maine, Annie had filled the long hours deprived of watching the boy she worshiped by conjuring up detailed images of their future. She must have imagined dozens of variations on their wedding, including the details of the bridal gown, the menu, even the music.

With a rueful smile, she closed her eyes and leaned her head against the cushions. What a dreamer she'd been.

And still a darn good dreamer, she thought, as she imagined she heard the faint strains of soft music. She let the pretty sound play in her head, smiling again, and her grip loosened on the magazine in her lap.

Thump. The lamb-and-rice-pilaf centerfold landed face-down on the floor, rousing Annie from her reverie. Her eyes popped open, and then as she automatically reached for the fallen magazine Annie realized there *was* music playing. Not just in her head, but somewhere on the Chase estate.

Intrigued, she stood and walked to her living-room window. It was full dark outside, and she expected her view to be dark, too, because this window overlooked the thick stand of oaks. But off in the distance, in the direction of the gazebo, Annie swore she could see tiny white lights—fairy lights they were called.

Annie bit her lip. Certainly, whatever was going on in the gazebo was none of her business. Unprecedented as it might be, perhaps Mr. and Mrs. Chase were having cocktails or dinner there. Maybe it was Logan and his almost-fiancée.

Possibly Griffin and a date.

Annie curled her fingers around the windowsill, bitten by a difficult-to-repress urge. *No.* She was too old to go sneaking through the woods to spy on him. For goodness sake, there was no reason to even believe it *was* him in the gazebo!

Still, that music was calling her. Staring into the night, she let the sound wash over her. Face it, juvenile impulse or no, she wouldn't get any work done until she'd satisfied her curiosity.

With a cursory glance at her jeans and dark sweatshirt, Annie slipped through her front door. She wouldn't disturb the privacy of whoever was using the gazebo, of course. That would be rude. Just a quick peek and then she'd be gone.

Weaving in and out of the trees, Annie felt like she

was ten years old again. The bark of the tree trunks had that same roughness under her fingertips, the damp leaves beneath her sneakers gave off the familiar fecund scent they always had.

Approaching the gazebo, she slowed. The music was louder now, but the lights were brighter, too. They *were* fairy lights, string after string of them, banding the roofline of the circular, white-lathe structure, running along the edge of the waist-high banister that enclosed it.

Though it was still shadowy inside, Annie could make out a table set with white linen and candles. The music had to be flowing from concealed speakers, yet Annie still didn't see anyone, or even any movement.

The pretty sight continued to draw her, and she dared moving one tree trunk closer. Keeping her body hidden behind it, she craned her neck for another peek. Who had planned such a romantic setting, and why?

"Hey, Annie." From the gazebo, a voice called softly into the darkness.

Annie froze. *No.* Griffin couldn't catch her spying now, not when he'd never caught her all those years before. He'd probably heard a noise and was just guessing, she assured herself. Using skills she hadn't practiced since childhood, she took a hasty, but silent step back. With her pride at stake, she refused to let him know he'd guessed right.

"Don't go."

And give him the satisfaction of her embarrassment? Yeah, right. Despite the quiet order, Annie scuttled backward again, but this time her behind sharply met the rough bark of a tree and she had to swallow her surprised yelp.

"I was hoping you'd hear my invitation," Griffin called out.

Annie froze again. His invitation? She crept forward once more and peered through the trees. The gazebo steps were in darkness. He must have been sitting on them before, because he was standing at the bottom of them now, wearing a dark suit.

"I know you're out there, honey."

Annie sighed, equal parts embarrassed and curious. Well, the gig was up now. Tilting up her chin, she stepped around her tree to face him.

They stood about ten feet apart. That music, something classical but light, Mozart, Annie thought, danced between them. The fairy lights decorating the gazebo lit Griffin's white shirt and flashed off his gold watch as he lifted his hand to her.

"Come here, honey," he said. "Come have dinner with me."

Annie pressed back against the tree. "What?"

He half turned to glance at the gazebo. "This is for you," he said.

She shook her head. "No."

"Yes." He walked toward her.

Her heart starting to pound, Annie backed tighter against the tree trunk. "Why?" she asked suspiciously.

Griffin didn't stop until he was standing directly in front of her. "Because you shouldn't feel cheap or used."

"I don't," she said quickly. Too quickly.

"Annie. Honey." He took in a long breath and

when he touched her cheek, a shiver rolled from where his fingertips touched her face to her toes. "I wish like hell I hadn't left you like I did that night. I wish like hell I had given you something besides regrets."

"Why?" Annie flattened her palms against the tree. "You have them."

He briefly closed his eyes. "Not the kind you think. And the biggest regret of them all is that I didn't give you what you deserve."

When he turned his head to look at the gazebo again, the lights set fire to his profile, edging him in gold. "I should have given you this. Before I took you to bed I should have given you romance."

Annie couldn't look away from him. "It's too late," she whispered.

"Let's pretend it's not." He cupped her face in his palms. He was gentle, oh, so gentle, and Annie's heart stuttered, stopped, started again.

He smiled gently. "Let's pretend for tonight that we've gone back in time. We've already had what comes later, so tonight let's have what should have come before."

He wanted her to come into the gazebo. He wanted to romance her. He wanted her, for tonight, to pretend. And Annie was afraid…because she was so darn good at pretending.

"Just for tonight." He drew his hands away from her face and shoved them in his pockets. "Just the romance, Annie. Nothing else."

It was a salve to his conscience. It was a sweet gesture. It was Griffin trying to repair something he thought he'd broken. It was horribly hard to say no.

So Annie didn't. Pursing her lips, she looked down at her sweatshirt and jeans. "I'm not dressed for romance."

He caught her hand, squeezed her fingers, let them go. "It doesn't matter what you wear."

She hesitated. "It does to me."

He nodded. "You'll come back?"

"Five minutes."

She took ten. In the three that it took to go from gazebo to cottage, she questioned her sanity. The next six minutes she spent shucking her jeans and searching her recently stocked closet for an outfit that would suit a romantic night in a fairy-lit gazebo.

The questions started up again as she slowly walked back to the gazebo wearing a pair of black boots, a long black skirt, and a black sweater set embellished with simple gold embroidery around the neckline. But when she saw Griffin again, waiting for her at the bottom of the steps, every doubt evaporated.

The corner of his mouth kicked up in that special, Griffin-only smile. He reached out his hand, and she looked at it, she looked at her own hand coming toward his. Fingers met fingers and her stomach jumped.

Griffin's smile died. "Annie," he said hoarsely. Then he shook his head, took a breath, put on that charming smile again. "This way."

It was silly to see those stairs as a path to destiny. It was fanciful and over-imaginative, a notion that thirteen-year-old Annie would have reveled in and that older-and-wiser Annie should have ejected from her mind. But it remained all the same, beyond her power to control.

He held her chair for her. He poured her wine, something that tickled her nose but that he said wasn't champagne. It entered her bloodstream like pure effervescence anyway, and after half a glass she worried that all her dreams might be written on her face.

She laughed at things he said. He served her food and she assured him it was delicious even though she didn't have any idea what she ate or any clear idea of its taste.

The charmed atmosphere appeared to affect Griffin, too. He touched her hands, her hair. He made to feed her something from his plate with his fingers, but when she obediently opened her mouth he only stared at her lips until she nudged his leg with hers.

Before they moved on to dessert, he had captured that leg between his. Their hands were clasped. They'd both stopped eating, or pretending to eat, and Annie was just looking at Griffin, taking pleasure in his touch, his face, his gaze on her. The music whirled around them. It was faster than Mozart now, wilder, something that gypsies might dance to, or maybe it was just that she felt gypsy-wild herself.

Her heart, every cell, the whole world felt wide open. The gazebo lights were like fairies flying around them. *We don't have a chance,* Annie thought. *There's too much magic in the air.*

"Annie." Griffin said her name like a warning.

Too late, Annie thought. "Yes."

"It was just supposed to be dinner tonight," he said, his eyes so serious, so dark. "I haven't changed."

"Yes," Annie answered.

When he stood, she stood, too. Their hands were

linked and she wasn't letting go. "Damn it, Annie," he said softly. "You know what I'm offering?"

"Yes." It was so easy to answer.

"Yes?" His fingers tightened on her hand.

"Yes."

They walked back to the cottage. He put his arm around her shoulders and drew her close to his body. Her head fitted perfectly into the cup of his shoulder. He kissed her temple, then slowed to kiss her lips, then halted altogether to deepen the kiss.

When his tongue filled her mouth, Annie's legs sagged. He laughed softly, swore he wouldn't kiss her again until they were closer to the bed, then broke his vow at her front door.

On that magic night, Cinderella brought the prince into her bedroom and he made gentle love to her. He cherished her in the darkness, slipping off her clothes, slipping his skin over her skin, slipping his body into hers.

Even as she moaned and quivered, under his expert touch moving inexorably toward climax, Annie sensed Griffin was still protecting her. More, she sensed he was still holding himself distant, but it was hard to analyze when the peaks were so sweet and so heart-poundingly high.

When it was over he cradled her in his arms. "I'm not going to be able to leave," Griffin said. "Not tonight."

Annie closed her eyes. *Yes.*

Chapter Eleven

"What should we do for your birthday?" Elena asked.

Annie reached for another sheet of the phyllo dough she had wrapped in a damp tea towel. "I can't think of anything until this catering job is finished." With the Chase anniversary only a few days away, Elena was helping Annie make the appetizers she'd store in the freezer until Sunday.

"That won't give us enough time to come up with something really special," Elena said.

The sound of the front door opening made Annie look up from the phyllo triangle she was folding. "Hello!" Griffin's voice called out.

"In here!" Annie called back, hoping she didn't sound as breathless as she felt. Since that night in the gazebo more than two weeks ago, Griffin had become a fixture in her life. In her bed.

As he usually did after a day at work, he strolled into her kitchen and as *it* usually did, Annie's heart went weightless. A deep breath didn't help. She glanced at the kitchen clock, thinking it was a positive sign that each day he was leaving the office earlier. Coming to her sooner.

"Ladies." Looking as self-assured and calm as always in a dark olive suit and white shirt, his tie loosened, Griffin smiled at Elena. Then he bent his head to kiss Annie's cheek.

He was bound to notice how hot it was, she thought. But he was too polite to mention it, just as he was too considerate to comment on how wildly her pulse was beating. No doubt he was aware of it, too, she could hear it in her own ears, for goodness sake, but Griffin never took advantage of what his nearness did to her.

At night, when he came down beside her in her bed, he was gentle, sweet, every breath, every touch, focused on her pleasure. He was a fantasy come to life and if just looking at him made her want him again, who could blame her?

Yes, she could understand why she wanted him. What she didn't understand was why she wanted more.

He stood behind her and placed his hands on her shoulders. "Are you going to be at this much longer?"

The firm sensation of his fingers made her think of how he had controlled her responses the night before, mercilessly stroking her until she cried out again and again. With her passion more subdued, only then had he come inside her body. There he controlled everything, too, controlling himself, slowly building the ecstasy again, slowly submerging them both into a heated pool of pleasure.

She had turned into his arms afterward, her heart still shaking inside her chest, while his had beat even and composed against her cheek.

"Annie?" He squeezed her shoulders. "Are you all right?"

"I'm fine." Of course she was. What kind of woman wanted more than the magic he offered? So what that he never seemed to lose himself the way she did? Annie swallowed and looked down at the bowls of spinach and feta cheese filling and then mentally counted how many appetizers they'd already made. "We have a couple more hours of work, I think."

"But you're just in time, Griffin," Elena said. "I'm trying to pin Annie down about her birthday celebration. It's the day after your parents' party, in case she's forgotten to tell you. Do you have any good ideas? A plan of your own up your sleeve?"

"Elena." Annie knew a test when she heard one. And she also knew Griffin was going to fail it.

He moved away from Annie, but his tranquil expression didn't flicker. "No plans."

Elena shot Annie a bland look. "Oh."

Annie suppressed her sigh. Elena wasn't any happier about Annie's relationship—no, her *association*—with Griffin than she had been the day after they had first made love. Annie tried smoothing over the awkward moment. "Can I get you something to eat?" she asked.

Griffin shook his head. "You don't have to feed me, Annie. I keep telling you that."

"Maybe she'd *like* to," Elena said sweetly. "It's the kind of thing people do for someone they, um—"

"What Elena means is that I'd *like* her to butt out," Annie interjected.

Griffin's eyebrows rose. "Well. On that note, I think I'll come back later." He paused. "If that's okay, Annie?"

She tried to hide her disappointment that he was leaving by training her gaze on the triangle she was folding. "Sure, come back later. If you feel like it, that is. If it's convenient. If you want to."

Elena made a rude noise that Annie ignored.

"Okay, then," Griffin said. "I'll see you later. Maybe."

"Okay." Annie looked up and hoped her smile was casual. Yet inviting. "But only if you feel like it," she said again.

This time, Elena waited until the front door had closed behind him. Then she made that rude noise again. "If he feels like it! If it's convenient!" She glared at Annie. "What's wrong with you?"

"There's nothing wrong with me."

Elena rolled her eyes. "That's right. I forgot. The thing that's wrong is wrong with *him*. I bet he hasn't given one thought to your birthday."

Annie dipped a brush in the nearby bowl of melted butter and swept it across the tops of the newly made appetizers. "Why should he?"

"Hello?" Elena rapped on the countertop with her knuckles. "Because the man's been sleeping with you every night, that's why."

"It doesn't mean we have a relationship. Or a future. I accept that. I'm fine with it." *I agreed to it.*

Elena made a sound—half moan, half groan.

"What?" Annie met her friend's gaze. "Don't tell me you think the only man I should make—have sex with is the man I'm planning to marry?"

Some of the exasperation left Elena's face. "This is going to sound weird, but I think I'd be less worried about you if you *were* just having sex with some guy. Unfortunately, instead, I think you *are* making love with the man you're planning to marry."

Annie shook her head. "You're wrong. That was a fantasy I had once upon a time, but I don't want to marry a fantasy." It was true, she realized. There was something wonderful and magical about what she and Griffin had right now, but it wasn't enough. Something about what they had wasn't real. It was almost as if *he* wasn't real enough.

"I don't want to see you with a broken heart."

Annie smiled. "You and me both. But truly, I'm fine with what we have. Content, even." A contentment that didn't rule out that what they had couldn't change for the better at some later time.

Elena mumbled something under her breath.

"What now?"

"I'm making a mental note to buy myself a new vacuum. Extra heavy duty for all those pieces I'm going to be picking up."

Annie laughed. "You're such a cynic."

"God, I hope so." Elena grinned. "That might be the nicest thing anyone's ever said to me."

"You're hopeless," Annie said, still laughing.

"Heartless," Elena corrected. "And you'll envy me for it someday."

That someday came only a few hours later, when Elena had left the cottage for home, and Annie was in the bathroom taking a shower. Without a heart, Annie wouldn't have nearly lost hers to a panic attack brought on when the bathroom door suddenly burst open.

"Where the hell were you?" She barely recognized Griffin's unnaturally harsh voice.

"What?" Even though the shower door was frosted, Annie automatically tried covering herself with her hands. "What's the matter?"

"You're all right?" he demanded.

"Of course I'm all right."

"You didn't answer your phone. Or the door."

"I've been in here awhile. What's the matter?"

Through the frosted glass, she couldn't see Griffin's face, only his dark figure standing in the doorway. "I was calling you," he said, his voice softer, but the words still almost an accusation. "And you didn't answer your phone."

Her pulse slowing, and more puzzled than concerned now, Annie stepped one last time beneath the water, then twisted the shower control to Off. Next, she opened the shower door just wide enough to pull her towel through, then snagged it from the nearby rack to quickly dry off.

With her pink towel tucked around her and the ends of her hair dripping on her shoulders, she stepped out of the shower. His posture and expression tense, Griffin stared at her from the open doorway. He'd changed from his suit and tie into black jeans and a long-sleeved black shirt. Instead of relaxing at the sight of her, his hands closed into tight fists, as if to stop himself from reaching out.

Annie's heart started hammering again. "What happened?"

His eyes flickered. "Nothing," he said. "I shouldn't have come. I should go home or to the office—"

"Something brought you here." She searched his face, trying to figure out what was bothering him. "Can't you tell me what's going on?"

"I should go," he said again, but he didn't move.

The weight of his gaze made her self-conscious. To give herself something to do, Annie tucked in the end of her towel more firmly between her breasts. Griffin's eyes followed her movement, then lingered on her exposed flesh.

Despite the open door that let the last of the shower's heat escape, the bathroom suddenly felt steamy. She swallowed again. "Griffin."

"Hm?" His gaze lifted, and there was something in his eyes that she hadn't seen before. They glittered, hard and bright, and Annie backed up until her towel-covered bottom met the porcelain sink.

"Wh-where've you been?" she asked.

"I...I didn't feel like going back to work so I met Logan at a bar."

Annie crowded closer to the sink, everything about Griffin's unusual intensity making her hot and nervous at the same time. Despite the towel, she'd never felt more naked in her life.

"I need—" She stopped, cleared her throat of its strange whisper, then started again. "I need to get my clothes on,'' she said firmly. Wearing something more than a pink rectangle would make it easier for her to face this strained mood of his.

''Okay.'' He still didn't move.

Sucking in a breath, Annie edged away from the sink. This was Griffin, she thought, scolding herself for her timidity, not some unfamiliar, unpredictable animal. But just as she reached the doorway, his arm shot out and he slammed his palm against the door-jamb, preventing her escape.

Annie jumped.

He didn't seem to notice. His glittering eyes didn't blink. ''You're sure you're okay?''

''I'm fine.'' *Fine.* She'd been saying it all night, hadn't she? Fine with their non-relationship. Fine that they had no future. Fine, fine, fine.

But it seemed like a big, fine, fat lie as she faced him now. She had sensed there was something running beneath that urbane, sophisticated mask he wore, but she didn't know how to handle what she saw in him at this moment—what she saw as the mask slipped.

Annie wished desperately she'd stayed in the shower, or, safer still, she wished she was fully dressed and hiding behind a tree somewhere, watching from a safe distance. ''You're scaring me.''

''Am I?'' His free hand reached out and one fingernail traced the curve of her shoulder. Annie's heart, her belly, clenched, the slight, erotic scratch so startlingly unlike the gentle, controlled moves he'd shown her before. ''But *I'm* the one who was scared tonight, Annie.''

He drew his fingernail over her skin again and she

trembled. "What scared you?" she asked, even though he didn't appear the least bit afraid. Just...edgy.

"Logan and I were sitting at the bar, watching the game." His touch continued to rasp over her skin, down to the barrier of her towel. He traced his fingernail across the top of her breasts. Annie wondered if she'd ever breathe again.

"The game ended, the ten o'clock news came on," he said. "There was another bank robbery this evening, Annie, just before closing time. The Reagan mask again. And someone was hurt."

"Hurt?" Annie choked, barely hearing the words or the tightness in his voice, as her skin reacted in jittery, hot and cold waves to that prickling, tickling finger.

"I needed to talk to you then, to hear your voice, but you didn't answer your phone." His finger stopped, right at the valley of her breasts, right where she'd tucked in the towel.

"I was in the shower," she said unnecessarily.

"Yeah," he said softly, though the softness was just a thin layer on top of rough, hard steel. "I know that now. But it made me crazy when I *didn't* know."

His fingers curled into the tuck of the towel, his knuckles hard against her bare skin. "I needed to hear your voice. I needed to see your face." Air was rasping in and out of his chest.

Annie was breathing hard, too. Nothing was gentle about Griffin now. Not his body, his touch, not his emotions.

"Damn it, Annie. I needed to touch you. I needed to touch you more than I needed to breathe."

His hand closed over her towel, and he jerked her closer to him. ''Damn *you,* Annie,'' he whispered harshly. With a choked groan and a choppy movement, he tore off her towel and bent to take her mouth.

Annie's head spun and heat ripped, jagged and burning hot from his mouth to her womb. The kiss was unrefined, unpolished, impolite even. But its crude power released something primal in her. When he thrust his tongue into her mouth, she widened for him instantly. When he slid his hands down to her naked hips, she was already pressing against his clothed body.

He groaned, his fingers biting into her flesh, and then the lights spun crazily. Her mouth still fused to his, she realized he was half-carrying, half-dragging her from the well-lit bathroom into her dark bedroom. At the last instant he tripped and she half fell, her belly landing against the mattress and her cheek against the pillow.

Before she could turn to pull him into her arms, he was on top of her, his clothed heat against her nude body. He groaned as his mouth came down, hot, on the side of her neck.

The hard ridge of his sex, covered by rough denim, brushed against the super-sensitive flesh of her soft buttocks. Desire shot up her spine and down, deep into her womb, crystallizing into something sharp and almost painful when he bit the lobe of her ear.

''Griffin,'' she said, but she didn't think he heard her, she didn't think he heard her breath catch either, as he rushed hot and hungry kisses across her shoulder blades, down her vertebrae. His knees on either side of her, he moved down her body, kissing, running his tongue along flesh she'd never considered erogenous.

His fingers bit into her hips again as he turned her over. Kneeling above her, he looked into her face, his eyes so dark they were almost a stranger's eyes. Holding her gaze, he reached down to tear off his shirt. Annie shivered, nervous, excited, so turned-on by watching those big hands, those long fingers move to his zipper.

Desire controlled him now, she thought. For once they were even.

But then, as if he couldn't wait any longer, Griffin dropped down on top of her. Rolling his hips to make a place for himself between her thighs, he bent to her mouth again. His teeth scraped against her bottom lip and the sensation, matched by the abrasion of coarse denim against her inner thighs, made Annie's head spin.

Griffin didn't linger long at her mouth, moving down to her breasts, caging them with his fingers and then lifting them so he could lick, suck, taste. Bite.

"Griffin!" Annie shuddered, and her hips pushed up toward him, wanting him, needing him.

His tongue swept over to the other breast, found the other nipple, and he bit down there, too. He groaned with pleasure.

His hand fumbled at his zipper. She heard the *vrriiip,* felt his knuckles abrade the inside of her thighs as he shoved down his jeans, his boxers. His mouth still tugging strongly on her nipple, he somehow rolled on a condom then fitted himself to her, thrust home.

She gasped. Griffin let go her nipple, his rough groan a hum against her breast. Her knees automatically raised, sending him deeper.

He stilled. She felt the war start up in him again, the last-gasp attempt to regain his civilized veneer. But then he groaned again and pumped into her, over and over and over.

He was without finesse this time. Without that fine control he had used every night to reel her in then wring her out. But her blood burned anyway, pulsing with every pump of his hips, with every harsh breath he sucked in.

"I need you," he muttered. "I need you, need you, need you."

Tilting her hips to take as much of him as she could, Annie ran her hands down his back. His skin was slick with sweat, and she reveled in the earthiness of it.

Then, chasing it with her palms, she felt his climax gather in his body. It surged up his hard thighs, rolled over his taut buttocks. With each thrust it gathered force in his hips. She held them between her hands, feeling the power buzzing like pure energy against her palms. Sweat dropped from his face onto her breasts and Annie shuddered in excitement.

"Oh, Annie." He thrust once more, deeper than ever before. Then again, deeper still.

Between her hands, the power burst like sparks against her fingers. Griffin jerked against her and once more groaned her name.

Usually, after making love, Griffin tenderly and considerately lifted his weight from her and gathered Annie in his arms. But this time, he didn't move.

This time, his body remained heavy against hers.

This time, Annie realized with a start, his body was still heavy *in* hers.

She cradled his head against her. He shifted, found her nipple with his mouth. Goose bumps washed over Annie's skin and the desire she'd banked burst instantly into flames. "Griffin, I—"

"More, Annie," he muttered. "Need more." He slipped partway out of her as he slid to lick and suck at her other breast. Then he moved farther still, moving his mouth under each breast, over her ribs, around her navel.

Nerve endings waved in wild abandon and Annie closed her eyes against a renewed, ragged spike of desire. It etched along her eyelids though, jagged and bright as lightning.

Griffin shifted again, but Annie was hardly aware of anything but the need recoiling in her womb. He lifted her knees, his shoulders brushed the inside of her thighs—his *shoulders?*—and then...then his mouth was on her.

Annie's eyes snapped open, even as her body trembled, hit again with another blast of jangling need. Griffin was between her legs, *feasting* on her body as if he couldn't get enough of it.

Heart slamming against her chest, Annie rose on her elbows, afraid of this new blast of desire, desperate to escape it. She tried twisting right, twisting left, retreating from his relentless—oh mercy, his *wickedly* good mouth—but Griffin's grip tightened on her hips. He looked up, and his naked chest was heaving with his indrawn breath. "Let me," he said, his voice harsh. "It wasn't enough. I need this, Annie. I need all of you."

He bent his head, licked again, found the place he could so expertly caress with his fingers. His tongue caressed it now, slid around it, toyed with it, with her, with every sane thought she'd ever had. Touch by touch, brick by brick, pleasure built, a high, encompassing wall of it.

Maybe she would have insisted he stop. Maybe she would have really moved away. But then he glanced at her once more and his face—his face so erotically framed by her thighs—was filled with a desire so wild, a need so hungry and so out of control that Annie surrendered, her head falling back.

Long strokes of his tongue. Short bursts of hot breath. The pleasure wall was all around her now, higher and stronger and Annie thought she might suffocate in the goodness of it. Griffin placed his hands on the insides of her thighs, splaying them wider. She lifted her head, uncertain again, and saw Griffin's face, untamed and intent.

Annie's breath caught. The wall, the pleasure, imploded.

In the hazy after-pleasure she saw him reach for another condom. Through half-opened eyes, she watched him roll it on his erection and then he drew her against him, her back to his chest.

"More," he said, by way of explanation, his voice guttural. Pulling her thigh on top of his, he thrust inside her.

Annie, who had thought herself bonelessly sated, felt a little thrill of pleasure. It was different like this, good with him hot and hard behind her.

Her eyes closed.

"I wanted you tonight." Griffin's mouth was against her ear and his breath was hot. Chills ran down her neck.

"I know," she whispered back. "And now you've had me."

He thrust upward. "No. Not just now, but when I came in from work. When you were in the kitchen."

Annie pressed back against him. "It would have been a little awkward with Elena there."

"I wanted you when I was sitting at my desk, when I was talking on the phone. Hell, Annie, I wanted you during a conference call with a supplier in Korea."

Annie gasped instead of giggling, because he'd found something to do with his hands, too. "You wanted me a lot."

"You're distracting me. I'm never distracted at work." His voice was harsh, his body hard inside hers, against hers. "You're making me forget things, Annie."

Annie had forgotten nothing. Not one minute of any of the dozens of daydreams she'd spun about Griffin over the years. His palm slid to her breast, cupped it. But this was better than all of them.

The reality of him was more than she could have dreamed. When he let down his guard, when he showed her the passion beating like another heart inside him, then she knew nothing had changed.

No. Everything had.

She loved Griffin. Not the boy she'd worshiped from afar. Not the Griffin Chase who she used to watch when she was thirteen, nineteen, twenty, as a riskless taste of romance.

She loved the man she had seen tonight, the man who had come to her tonight with need glittering in his eyes.

Her nipples pearled under his touch and again she pressed back against his body. He drove inside her urgently, his breath sawing in and out.

"More," he muttered again, pushing her leg higher.

Her body and her heart opened. More. Everything. All.

She was in love with him.

Chapter Twelve

Annie propped her feet on her mother's coffee table and stared at them, wondering why they appeared shod in leather when she felt like she was wearing glass slippers.

She'd been walking that carefully.

Knowing she loved Griffin and knowing he wouldn't thank her for it was like crossing eggshells in Cinderella's shoes. After an entire day of such wearying pressure, she'd escaped her cottage to the safety of her mother's apartment. This way, if Griffin didn't come looking for her, she wouldn't know it. This way, if he didn't call her, as he hadn't called her all day, she wouldn't have to spend the evening staring at a silent phone.

"Here we are." Her mother placed a tray of tea and cookies beside Annie's feet. "You look like you need something to keep you awake."

Annie hadn't slept at all the night before. After their final bout of passion, Griffin had crashed in her bed, his arm heavy and possessive over her waist. With his heart pumping steadily against her back, she'd tracked the passing hours by staring at the hands of his watch. The expensive, elegant watch that matched so well the elegant man he was.

But underneath his golden veneer something else ticked away, an intensity, needs that she suspected he wouldn't be happy about having revealed.

She was right.

Six hours and seven minutes after he'd driven himself into her body one last time, six hours and seven minutes after she'd confronted the truth—that she was in love with a man who hid parts of his nature just as she used to hide behind trees—he'd slipped out of her bed.

The impending dawn was enough to dimly light the bedroom, yet he'd never glanced her way. If he knew she was awake and watching him leave her, he'd hidden that from her, too.

She hadn't said anything to him either, of course, afraid she'd give her love away. Annie had known then, as she knew now, that the only thing she could do about the situation was wait. Maybe Griffin would accept more from her some day. Maybe he'd find in himself the kind of commitment that her feelings would demand.

Clack. The sound of a saucer hitting the tabletop made Annie start. She looked into the sympathetic face of her mother.

"Want to talk about it?" Natalie asked.

Annie shook her head. "Nothing to talk about,"

she said lightly. Her mother would worry and Annie was doing enough worrying for the both of them.

"Is it that other bank robbery?"

Annie blinked. Goodness. Consumed by her own dilemma and thoughts, she'd almost forgotten about the robbery that had precipitated Griffin's raw mood.

"No. Have you heard any more about the woman wounded, though?" The sketchy morning newspaper account had said a teller had been injured by the Ronald Reagan robber when she'd tried to delay him by holding onto the bag of money.

Natalie poured her own cup of tea. "It was a superficial knife wound."

Annie frowned. "A knife? No gun this time?"

"No. I saw an interview on TV with the teller. She said it was definitely a knife."

Annie shuddered. A knife wasn't any less frightening than a gun. Would the teller change her life as Annie had because of the incident? "Let's talk about something else," she said, looking around the room. "Any more postcards from Aunt Jen?"

Her mom nodded. "That sister of mine got all the stubbornness in the family."

Annie smiled. "Oh, I don't know, Mom. You're holding out pretty well."

"Because I don't want to move to San Diego!"

Annie paused, struck by the uncompromising vehemence in her mother's voice. "Is there something wrong, Mom?"

"Of course not." Her mother looked away. "I just wish I could get through to Jen."

Annie picked up her cup and saucer and held them close to her nose, letting the fragrant steam wash over her face. "Of course I love having you nearby, Mom, but please, I hope you're not hanging around Strawberry Bay just for me. I'm all grown-up you know."

Her mom still didn't meet Annie's eyes. "It's not that. It's…not just you."

Maybe falling in love gave Annie extra perception. Maybe it had fine-tuned her heart, because she heard something in her mother's voice, saw something in her mother's face that was suddenly unnerving. "Why *are* you staying, Mom?"

Her mother vaguely waved her hand, but it was her gaze that gave her away. It slid to the small table by the window where the family pictures had rested for as long as Annie could remember.

Her mother looked at her father's picture.

Annie sipped her tea to moisten her mouth gone suddenly dry. Was her mother still in love with her father? Not one single recollection of him was stored in Annie's memory banks, but at twenty, her mother had run away from her parents' house with him, had a child—Annie—with him when she was thirty, and when Natalie was thirty-three, Annie's father had run away from *them*.

Thirteen years she'd lived with the man. Twenty-two she'd lived without him.

Yet she still kept his photograph displayed and dusted it every day.

Annie swallowed. "Why did you and my father settle in Strawberry Bay in the first place, Mom?"

Her mother let go a little laugh. "It's where your father's car finally gave up the ghost. It was a Volkswagen Beetle that had once been in a car accident. Both headlights were gone and a door was bashed in.

You had to crawl through the window to sit on the passenger side.''

The amusement in her voice died. ''At first I was terrified that your grandfather, my father, would find us here. Later, though, Jen told me he never looked. He was that angry with me for quitting college and running away with a long-haired, guitar-toting boy.''

Annie looked at the photo her mother was so fond of. Her father's hair hung to his shoulders, and he looked at the camera through a pair of wire-rimmed glasses. ''Where'd he go, Mom?'' She'd never asked the question before. Not why, either, always sensing it was a subject too painful for her mother to speak about.

Natalie shook her head. ''I don't know.''

''But...'' Annie didn't know why she thought she had the right to pry now, but she couldn't stop herself. ''But you loved him, Mom?''

''Yes.'' Natalie was focusing at the photo. ''I love him.''

Cold crept down Annie's back, even with the steam from the hot tea warming her face. *I love him,* her mother had said. Not I *loved* him, but I *love* him.

She set down her teacup and saucer, a realization gathering force. ''Mom...''

Her mother glanced at her, glanced away.

Scattered pieces of the puzzle began assembling themselves in Annie's brain. A few years ago, Natalie's father had died. Despite his disapproval of her marriage, he'd left her a comfortable inheritance that had allowed her mother to retire from the housekeeping work that was becoming so difficult due to arthritis.

While she could have bought her own home, Natalie instead chose to rent this small apartment near downtown Strawberry Bay. Annie remembered her saying it was just a few steps away from the apartment she had once lived in with Annie's father.

Her mother had arranged her old furniture in almost exactly the same pattern it had been in the cottage. A pattern Annie now strongly suspected was the same as it had been when her father had lived with her mother. And even though Natalie had been overjoyed at a reunion with her sister several years back, she had never once seriously considered taking Aunt Jen up on her invitation to move to sun-drenched San Diego.

"Mom—" Annie swallowed, started again. It was as hard to believe as it was to say. "Mom, are you waiting for him to come back?"

Her mother acted as if she hadn't heard Annie's incredulous question.

"Mom, it's been more than twenty years."

Her mother's voice was low, almost a whisper. "This is where he'd know to find me."

Annie gaped. No. It just couldn't be. "But...but it's been so *long*." That her mother would put her life on hold, that she would *wait* for so many years, was...what? Sad? That didn't seem a strong enough word.

"You can't choose who you love," Natalie said.

But you could choose how you *acted!* You could choose to track him down, you could choose to actively find someone else, you could hold onto your pride and you could even hold onto hope, Annie supposed. But to wait, just wait, for all that time seemed like no kind of life at all.

It's the kind of life you just signed on for, a little voice whispered.

No. Waiting for Griffin to want her love wasn't anything close to what her mother was doing. Her mother was fantasizing, daydreaming her life away.

Just what you did all the years before.

Appalled at the truth of that, Annie closed her eyes. But she wasn't like her mother. She wasn't! She would never patiently wait over twenty years for her love to be returned.

And yet…

And yet she was afraid she just might.

Waiting, hiding, hoping but not *doing* were the hallmarks of Annie's life.

Her old life, she insisted to herself. The life that she'd vowed to change with her cheek against that gritty linoleum floor and the caustic smell of pine cleaner in her nose. She'd sworn then to seek sensation, experience—no. What she'd sworn then was to seek love.

Annie's eyes opened and she looked at her mother. She loved her mom, loved her with every ounce of her being, but she refused to follow in her footsteps. In those moments on the floor at the Strawberry Bay Savings and Loan, she'd learned something.

Life was too short not to say what was in your heart. It was too short not to ask for what you wanted.

Annie stood up. "I'm going home now."

Natalie smiled sadly. "Have I disappointed you?"

Annie shook her head. "I love you, Mom." It was

just that there was someone else she needed to say those three words to.

Annie stood on the well-lit and tennis-court-sized doorstep of the Chase home—the Montgomery Mansion—trying to recall ever using the front entrance. As a girl, she'd flitted in and out of the side door that led into the kitchen. She'd learned to roller-skate in the cavernous garage when Mr. and Mrs. Chase were out in their mammoth luxury cars. She'd saved herself from falling by clutching the fenders of the classic Mustang Griffin drove in high school.

She knew every nook and cranny of the inside of the house, too. Her first job was as an assistant to her mom. At wages better than babysitting money thanks to the Chases, she'd spent four summers saving for cooking school by dusting, polishing and waxing.

But the front door was new territory and its unfamiliar barrier was what had to be making her heart rattle around in her chest and her palms sweat. Gulping a breath, she visualized her mother—over two decades of waiting!—and then stabbed at the doorbell with a finger she pretended wasn't trembling.

Mrs. Kutz, her mother's replacement, answered the door. "Annie!" She smiled broadly. "I was just thinking we needed to go through the party details again."

As her mother had, Mrs. Kutz worked from one in the afternoon until ten at night, with an hour off for dinner. There were house-helpers who worked in the morning and groundskeepers who worked all day, but for entertaining purposes, Mrs. Chase liked her housekeeper on the job in the afternoon and evening.

Annie smiled back, hoping her nervousness wasn't showing. "Maybe we can set up an appointment for tomorrow afternoon. But now I'm here to see…Griffin."

The housekeeper didn't even blink, her training wouldn't allow her to express surprise, of course. "Let me show you to the library then. Mr. Griffin and Mr. Logan and Miss Cynthia are having dessert with Mr. and Mrs. Chase."

Though Annie knew the house as well as she knew her own, she obediently followed Mrs. Kutz's broad back. Mr. Griffin, Mr. Logan and Miss Cynthia, she thought, Mr. and Mrs. Chase. She needed to see, to talk to *Griffin*, only *Griffin*. Her footsteps slowed as doubt fed on insecurity, which then fed on more doubt. She could beat a hasty retreat. Call him on the phone.

Heck, a telegraph would do.

The idea came too late. Mrs. Kutz turned the knob of the paneled library door. "Here you are," she said. As the door swung open, Annie sucked in a long, calming breath.

Mrs. Chase looked up first. "Annie." Wearing a violet-colored, form-fitting knit dress, she was seated in a wing chair beside a low-burning fire. "Come in, dear."

Annie crossed gleaming hardwood until her feet sank into the plush Oriental carpet. "Good evening. I—I hope I'm not disturbing you."

Her gaze passed over everyone in the room. Cynthia Halstead sat, thin, beautiful and bored-looking, in a chair that matched Mrs. Chase's. The men, Jonathon Chase and his two tall sons, still in coats and ties, were gathered around the billiard table.

Mr. Chase acknowledged her presence with a salute from his after-dinner glass of Scotch. Logan smiled at her.

Griffin simmered. "Annie," he said.

Just her name. And the deep tones in his voice made her think of the dark night and his body deep in hers. A shiver trickled down Annie's spine. This was the man she loved.

"Did you have a question about the party?" Mrs. Chase asked.

Annie's gaze jerked toward her. "No. I—"

"Are you catering the party then, Annie?" Cynthia sounded as bored as she looked.

Annie swallowed, then darted a look at Griffin. "Well, yes, but—"

"I loved that dish you made for Sondra Ward's baby shower." Cynthia used one rose-colored nail to push her white-blond hair behind her ear, looking slightly more alive now that they were talking about food. "What's it called again?"

"Cheese enchiladas." Looking at the other woman's supermodel slimness, Annie decided against mentioning that Cynthia's memory might be better if she ate more often. Or just plain more. "I'm here to—"

"What are you serving at the party?" Cynthia slid to the edge of her chair.

"What is this party you're babbling about, Cynthia?" Mr. Chase said. "You're not giving Annie a chance to talk."

Annie wondered if Logan would defend his almost-fiancée, but it was Mrs. Chase who spoke next, her voice coming coolly from her place by the fire. "*Our* party, Jonathon. Our anniversary party this Sunday."

Mr. Chase frowned, then took a sip of his Scotch. "Is this on my calendar?"

"Yes, Jonathon." Mrs. Chase's calm expression concealed any other feelings. "And no, before you ask, you won't be out of town, or on your way out of town, or even missing a crucial golf tournament."

Logan was shaking his head, his expression amused. "Forty years, Dad. You remember that, don't you?"

"Dad remembers anything he chooses to remember." Griffin interjected. "That is, anything important to him."

Jonathon Chase either didn't hear the edge to his elder son's voice or chose to ignore it. "It's Annie I'm remembering right now. She still hasn't had a chance to tell us why she's here."

Annie had a sudden wild and giddy impulse to blurt it out. Right here, in front of on-the-edge-of-starvation Cynthia, in front of Mr. and Mrs. Chase, who apparently always treated each other like strangers.

If she confessed she was in love with their son, Mr. Chase would probably pour another finger of Scotch and go back to his billiards. Mrs. Chase would remain frozen by the fire. Cynthia was probably too hungry to give the subject her attention and Logan wouldn't care.

Only Griffin would react, and she had no idea how.

That's what she'd come to find out. "I'm here to see Griffin," she said.

"Ah." Mr. Chase turned back to his Scotch. "A legal matter, I suppose."

Apparently satisfied, Mrs. Chase smiled vaguely. Logan gave his attention to the felt-covered table. Cynthia wondered aloud when the dessert would show up.

Obviously Griffin hadn't told anyone he was having regular sex with the housekeeper's daughter.

But maybe if they could see his wary face as he strolled toward her, they might figure it out. His hand closed around her elbow, the touch probably appearing casual and polite, though Annie felt the heat of his fingers through her sweater, her skin, to the very nerves underneath. She shivered.

"Where would you like to talk?"

At the moment, Annie couldn't speak at all. She shrugged.

"Are you too cold to go outside?" He nodded toward the French doors that led to the surrounding veranda.

Annie shook her head. Griffin led her outside, shutting the French doors firmly behind him. A matching pair of wicker-and-cushion couches were positioned nearby and he dropped her arm to make his way toward one. "What do you want, Annie?"

He was on edge, she guessed, because he didn't know how to handle what had happened between them last night. She licked her lips, trying to tamp down her anxiety.

"I didn't say goodbye to you this morning," she said softly. The fact was, he hadn't said goodbye to her either, but she had to start the conversation somehow.

Standing beside the couch, he lifted his hand, dropped it. "No big deal."

She took a breath. A chance. "Last night was a big deal."

He stilled. He was only an outline in the dark, but she could tell that she'd struck a soft spot. "I'm sorry if I hurt you."

"Hurt me?"

His hand lifted again, dropped. "If I was too…rough."

An echo of his voice, *more, more,* he'd whispered, sounded in her head. Distracted her from the task at hand, she shook her head and spoke quickly. "You had to know I liked it."

"Well."

"I like it every way," Annie said. "Every way with you." She swallowed. "Love it, as a matter of fact."

He laughed without humor. "Guess I can't complain about that."

Annie willed her heartbeat to slow. "No," she said. This wouldn't be so bad, she reminded herself. This was Griffin. "You shouldn't complain at all."

Even in the dark she thought she could tell his shoulders had relaxed a little. "So why are you here? You're welcome, of course, but I get the feeling something's on your mind."

You walked into that one, buddy. Annie grimly smiled.

"It's…" She trailed off, unsure where to begin. From the beginning. Yes.

"It's about the robbery," Annie said.

He stiffened again. "What's the matter? Has something happened—"

"No, no." Annie put out her hand. "Nothing like that. I meant to say that the robbery changed me."

"How so?" Wariness had returned to Griffin's voice.

"You saw me afterward. Throwing my shoes…and such."

"You said you didn't want to wait any more."

Annie nodded. "That's right. That's exactly right." She swallowed. "I hadn't had much experience with men, you see."

"I *know*."

His voice rasped against her in the dark. Annie shivered again. "Well. Right. Of course. But when I was lying on the floor of the bank, I wasn't really thinking about sex."

"Somehow I'm not surprised," Griffin said dryly. "It would seem natural that something else…say, survival…might be upmost in your mind."

"I was thinking about love," Annie blurted out.

There was a long, pregnant pause.

"Annie…"

He was warning her again. She knew it. Her heart sank.

"Give me the chance to say the words, Griffin," she whispered.

He was shaking his head. "You said you wouldn't. You said you didn't expect anything more."

"I had a traumatic experience," she said quickly. "I reevaluated my life. And I discovered what I was lacking was love. I'd never loved a man before."

He took a step back. "It's doesn't have to be me."

"Of course it doesn't." She hesitated. "It's just that it *is* you."

He groaned. "Damn it, Annie. You're too young, sex is too new, it's hormones or—"

"It's *you,* Griffin."

"This wasn't supposed to happen." His voice had a desperate edge.

Annie didn't think that was a good sign. "I'm sorry. I know this is unexpected—"

"Unwelcome."

She winced. "Whatever. But I want you to understand I'm not expecting you to love me back."

"Really?" he said suspiciously.

"Not on my timetable, anyway." Annie tried to arrange her thoughts clearly, even as her heart seemed to expand in her chest. "That wouldn't be fair, would it? But I can't just sit on my feelings, Griffin. I've been hiding in corners and behind trees all my life, and this was something I just can't hide, too."

"Annie—"

"Let me just ask, okay?" Her voice had gone hoarse with suppressed emotion, with fear, probably. But she forced the words out anyway, thinking of her mother tending that dustless photo. "Life is too short to wait, Griffin. Too short to wait for someone to come back. Too short to wait for someone to love you back if they never will."

She took one last, deep breath. It was a risk, laying her feelings out for the man who had never wanted commitment, who had always had a new woman in his life.

"So. I'm in love with you, Griffin. What do you say? Could you love me one day? It doesn't have to be tomorrow, or even next week, but sometime in the next year, or even the next month, or—''

"Annie." He was suddenly in front of her, his hands on her shoulders. "Annie, stop."

There was a high whine in her ears. "I'm babbling. You see, tonight I went to my mother's and when I was there she served me tea and my Aunt Jen had sent her another postcard and—''

"I'm not going to love you, Annie. I'm sorry, but I'm not."

Her heart that had been near to popping out of her chest, suddenly deflated. The whine in her ears abruptly cut off, leaving only loud, dark, sad silence. "Okay," she heard herself say.

"Annie…"

The ugliest of Annie's insecurities reared its head. "Is it because I'm the housekeeper's daughter?"

His fingers bit into her skin. "God, Annie, *no.*"

"Fine. Okay." She tried to move away from him, but his grip tightened again on her shoulders.

"I hate that I'm hurting you. But damn it, Annie, I told you how it was with me."

"I know." She truly could hear the regret in his voice. She'd known she was taking a chance imagining he would be interested in settling on just one woman. On her. Griffin had never wanted love and marriage.

He groaned again, then spun her around, so that she faced the library. With Annie and Griffin standing in the darkness and his family in the well-lit room, it was as if they watched the Chase family on a television screen. Though they were standing outside in a cool spring night, the atmosphere inside the library appeared chillier.

"We don't do it well," Griffin said. "Tell me you can see that."

Mrs. Chase looked toward her husband, said something, but it was obvious he didn't hear her. Or didn't listen. It took Logan jabbing his father with his cue stick to get Jonathon Chase to respond to his wife.

Griffin swore under his breath. "Would I wish for forty years of that? There's no closeness, no warmth."

But he'd been close to her last night. He'd revealed a passion that wasn't the least bit cool. He couldn't give up all the women in his life for that? For her? "Last night—"

"That wasn't me," he said harshly.

So harshly, she stepped away from him. So harshly, she thought he just might be right.

"Listen to me, Annie," Griffin said, his voice still rough. "I don't love you. God help me, I *won't* love you."

Chapter Thirteen

If the weather for his parents' anniversary party had taken a cue from Griffin's mood it should have been dreary clouds and damp air. But since the cosmos hadn't been paying him much mind lately, he admitted, it came as no surprise that that late Sunday afternoon was California perfect. It was blue skies and sunny warmth that ripened the berries in the fields surrounding Strawberry Bay to a sweet, juicy red.

Everything was springlike at the Chase estate, too, from the linen-draped, flower-topped tables set out on the verandas, to the festive mood of the guests, women in pastel silks, men in white jackets.

Everything, that is, except for Griffin's mood and his parents' marriage. There wasn't one warm thing about either one.

Shoulder-to-shoulder with Logan, Griffin contemplated his mother and father as they stood at the entrance to the gardens greeting their guests. Of course they were gracious—why even now his mother was smiling at that weaselly Joey Delvecchio who was with his Uncle Louis the car dealer—but there was no tenderness between his parents, no shared smiles, no understanding looks. His father's single-minded focus on Chase Electronics had never allowed a closeness to grow.

Add that lousy example to his own half-hearted and ridiculously ill-timed attempt at commitment so many years ago, and Griffin could feel pretty good about being honest with Annie about not loving her. Well, no, he felt like hell for hurting her, but still it had been the right thing to do. It was only a temporary sting she felt, he was sure.

He'd only been her fantasy, after all. The reality of him, the real Griffin who women found charming but distant, friendly but too career-focused, wasn't someone she would love.

"Geez, Grif, the wheels in your head are churning so loud I can hear them from here," Logan said.

Griffin glanced at him. Though he wasn't a big drinker, Logan was on his third whiskey and the party had barely begun. "What's with you?" Griffin said, nodding at the drink. "And where's Cynthia?"

"Cynthia and I broke up," Logan said casually. "As for the whiskey—" he deftly turned his wrist to dump the liquid in a nearby planter overflowing with flowers, "—it just gives me an excuse to bait the bartender."

Griffin's puzzlement cleared when he checked out who was standing behind the bottles of champagne and other liquors. Elena. "If I were you I'd make sure she doesn't bait your glass with poison," he murmured, then his brother's first comment registered. "Wait a minute. You broke up with Cynthia, you said?"

"Yeah." Logan's gaze stayed fixed on Elena. "Yeah, I did."

Griffin sighed. "I suppose I understand, though you and Cynthia have been going together for a long time. Mother and Dad's marriage has shown me what I can't have, too."

"Can't have?" Logan's gaze flicked briefly to Griffin's face, then back to Elena. "It's shown me what I was almost lazy enough to settle for. Can't have is an entirely different proposition."

Griffin stared. "But—"

"Excuse me." Toting his empty glass, Logan strolled off in the direction of the bar.

A figure came into Griffin's line of vision. Dressed in a thin V-necked sweater and knee-length lace skirt, both the color of champagne, Annie fussed with the placement of a platter of hors d'oeuvres on one of the long tables set with food. Suddenly, she looked up, right at him, and it was the same as the day he'd seen her climb out of the paddy wagon at the police station.

Familiarity, fate, an odd, instinctive sense of her trouble being his. He wanted to shake it off, he wanted to look away, but there were shadows beneath her eyes and he'd put them there.

It had been three days since he'd seen her, three days since he'd told her he wouldn't love her. It had been damn difficult to stay away because his need to watch over her hadn't abated, but the party preparations had not only kept her busy, but safe behind the gates of the Chase estate.

He couldn't stay away now, he thought, slowly walking toward her. When he reached her, he dredged up a smile. "Everything looks wonderful, Annie."

Her breasts rose with a quick breath. "Thanks."

"You okay?" he asked.

Her breasts rose again. Griffin tried not to think of that night when he'd found her in the shower. He tried not to think of the dark passion he'd uncontrollably unleashed on her.

"I'm fine," Annie said, her voice stiff. "You?"

Another voice joined their stilted conversation. "Griffin's always fine!"

He turned to see the recognizable smile of his longtime friend Nicole and then was hugged by her notso-recognizable, strangely plump body. She released her hold on him, giving him a chance to step back.

"You're pregnant," he said.

Her hand flew to her chest in surprise, but her voice teased. "Griffin! Your powers of observation have positively grown! I'm pregnant all right, eight months pregnant."

"Congratulations."

"You could have congratulated me sooner if you'd bothered to call and tell me you'd returned to the States early."

Griffin shrugged sheepishly. "Sorry. I've been… busy."

"Always busy, that's you. If you have a thought in your head beyond your precious company, I've rarely seen it." Her smile took some of the sting out of her truthful words and then her gaze flicked toward Annie. "Introduce me?"

"Oh. Of course." He gestured across the table of food. "Nicole Macy, this is Annie Smith. Annie, Nicole."

"Annie Smith, the caterer?" Nicole asked. "Annie who grew up on the estate?"

Annie nodded.

Nicole leaned over the table, her rounded belly threatening to flatten the platter of appetizers. "I'm Nicole who got Griffin to agree to be my man of honor."

Annie's eyes widened. "You did? I mean...he did?"

Nicole nodded smugly. "A coup, I tell you. I don't believe there's another woman alive who could get this man to the altar, but *I* did it."

"Well, I'm certain you're right," Annie murmured stiffly. "He's quite the playboy."

At Annie's cool tone, Nicole's gaze jumped from Annie to Griffin and back again. She frowned. "Is there—"

An insistent voice calling her name made her break off.

She looked over the crowd of partygoers, waved, then looked back at Annie and Griffin. "Something's going on here," she said. "But I'll have to figure it out later." When that voice called her name again, she gave them one last distracted smile and hurried off.

Griffin turned back to Annie, who was minutely adjusting the platter again. "That's Nicole," he said, for lack of anything better.

"Mmm." Annie took a step to the left to line up a row of gleaming silver forks. "I thought you'd made the whole man of honor thing up."

His eyebrows rose. "What?"

She kept her eyes lowered. "And that proposal business. Guess I was wrong about that, too."

Unsure why she'd think he'd lie about it, Griffin shoved his hands in his pockets. "Well, yeah. Nicole was the woman I almost proposed to."

"That would have been your child she was carrying."

"I suppose." Though the idea of being married to Nicole seemed ludicrous to him now. "But she knew better."

Annie looked up. "What do you mean?"

"She knew I was...distant. Wrapped up in my work. Lousy husband material."

Annie rubbed her forehead. "I still don't get it. You *wanted* to be husband material?" she asked, as if she couldn't fathom it.

"I thought I told you that before." He smiled ruefully. "I wasn't as smart as I am now. I saw my parents' marriage and was determined that it wouldn't be the same for me. I thought I could settle down, have a happy, committed relationship. The irony is I chose Nicole. If I'd been the kind of man who should marry—who understood what went into a good marriage—I would have recognized the right feelings weren't there. That she cared for someone else."

Annie stared at him. "I don't believe it."

"I told you I wasn't very smart. But the women in my life have always been. They complain I'm distant, too wrapped up in my work." He was his father, Jonathon Chase, all over again. "Sound like someone we know?"

"You think you're like your father."

Griffin shrugged; of course he did. "Women complain I never let my heart show, when the truth is, like my father before me, I don't have one."

There was a moment of silence, then Annie whispered hoarsely. "I thought you were rejecting *me*."

Griffin's gut clenched. "What?"

"The other night, when I told you…when I told you how I felt, I thought you were rejecting me."

"No, Annie!" He made a grab for her hand, found it, then refused to let her pull away. "It's not about you. I…care for you."

"But you could never bring yourself to marry me."

Her fingers flexed in his, but he wouldn't let them go. "No. How could I do that? What the hell do I know about making someone happy?"

"Because of your father, your parents."

He squeezed her hand. "Because of them, because of me. What does it matter? I just know that I like things…light."

"Shallow," Annie corrected. "Deep is scary. Deep means you might get hurt."

"I'm not afraid, Annie!" A spurt of anger heated his blood. He closed his eyes to control the emotion, then released her fingers to run both hands through his hair. "Oh, hell, so I am. But not for me. You've got that part wrong. I'm afraid I'd hurt you, Annie, like my father hurts my mother. I'd never forgive myself for that."

She backed away then, looking at him as if he'd stabbed her in the heart.

He groaned. "Annie—"

She whirled and ran.

Swiping her cheeks with the back of her hands, Annie rushed away from Griffin and the sounds of the party. *I need just a minute,* she told herself. *Just a minute to get myself together.*

Of course she ran toward the stand of oaks.

It was the haven, the refuge, the fantasy world of her childhood. It was here she'd dreamed every dream and it seemed fitting that here she would go to accept that the most important dream of all had died.

Annie found herself at the empty gazebo. The fairy lights were still strung about the structure, but their magic was gone. Mounting the steps, Annie ran her hand along the stair rail and the wood felt cold and lifeless.

Like her heart. At least like she thought it would be once she managed to squeeze out all its sadness.

Closing her eyes, Annie recalled that enchanted night with Griffin. Every look they'd exchanged had deepened the spell, every touch had made him only more fascinating.

She'd talked big that night, telling him she was willing to accept what little he had to offer. But she'd been dreaming big, too, every moment in his arms cementing the romantic fancy that she could have him forever.

That she *would* have him forever.

Even on the veranda the other night, when he'd turned her to watch the Chase family's cold tableau, and said he wouldn't love her, she hadn't believed him. Deep down, she'd believed it was merely reluctance speaking for him—the proverbial playboy resisting the net.

She thought he only needed to get used to the idea. But now she knew the truth.

Because he'd always been so focused on the family company just like his father, he'd avoided commitment. It wasn't marriage, or even Annie he was resisting, but being responsible for making someone else happy.

Annie buried her face in her hands. She was good at wishing. Maybe if she did it hard enough, wanted it badly enough, she could wish herself back to that cold, pine-scented linoleum floor. This time, she'd stay belly-down. They'd have to pry her off the floor, and once they did, she would know not to make any stupid vows.

She'd go back to her safe, comfortable, in-the-corner, behind-the-tree existence.

At least then she'd have a whole heart.

Swiping at another rush of useless tears, Annie forced herself back down the stairs. There was no time for crying. Broken heart or no, she needed to get back to the party.

On the last step, her shoe caught on an exposed nail. Trying to tug it free, Annie jerked up her knee, only succeeding in liberating the high heel from the sole and the ankle strap from the side of the shoe.

Annie glared at what had been expensive—and was now ruined. "I should have known I'd be better off with discount," she muttered, then swung in the direction of her cottage instead of the party, limping on the unevenly matched shoes.

Walking through the woods in the half-broken pair

wasn't easy, but it only became more difficult once she reached the pea-gravel path surrounding the cottage. Aware she needed to hurry back to the party, Annie put her head down to quickly pick her way, the heelless, strapless shoe slapping uncomfortably.

Clunk!

Startled by the unexpected bang of metal against metal, the sound the slam of the lid of a car trunk, Annie's head jerked up. Her still-rushing feet slid on the gravel and the uneven shoes made gaining purchase impossible. With a stifled cry, Annie fell forward.

Lying face-down on the path, her cheek against the cold gray pebbles, Annie took a moment to catch her breath. It was enough time for a pair of black men's shoes to venture into her field of vision.

Familiar shoes.

The gravel's cold invaded her body.

Annie pressed her belly against the ground, but she couldn't stop her gaze from traveling upward. Ankles, knees. Metal. The metal of a gun pointing right at her.

Annie squeezed her eyes shut. *No.*

But when she opened them, the shoes were still there. Familiarly tied. The gun was still there, too.

"What are you doing, Joey?" Annie asked, her voice like a croak. "Why do you have that gun?"

The gun was shaking and so was Joey's voice. "I *knew* you recognized me. I just knew it."

Griffin wandered toward the bar, trying to decide on the quickest method of getting drunk. An altered state of consciousness—hell, *un*consciousness—was the only way he was going to forget the stricken look on Annie's face.

The broken dreams in her eyes.

It wasn't his fault! He'd been trying to convince himself of that for the last fifteen minutes. From the beginning, she'd said her eyes were open.

Those beautiful, star-filled eyes.

He shrugged the image away and stepped up to the bartender. Elena. Bracing himself for one of her verbal sword thrusts, he grimly smiled. "Whiskey. Neat."

Instead of smiling—or what he'd thought more likely, sassing—back, she lowered her eyebrows in a worried frown. "Have you seen Annie?"

He ignored the odd lurch in his chest. "Well, yeah. A while ago."

"No. I mean recently. In the past few minutes."

He wrapped his hand around the glass of whiskey she passed over. The inch of amber liquid wasn't enough. "Make it a double, would you?" He glanced around the terrace, looking for Annie's graceful figure dressed in soft gold. "She's probably in the kitchen."

Elena splashed more whiskey in his glass. "She's not there either. The college crew that she hired to serve have been looking all over for her. They want to know where she put the rest of the shrimp."

He knocked back a mouthful of the alcohol. "We had a…conversation," he admitted. "Maybe she was a little upset."

Elena rolled her eyes. "Way to go, Romeo."

"Hey—"

"Never mind." Elena impatiently cut him off. "I

don't care what you said. I still don't think she'd leave the party for long.''

Something lurched in his chest again. ''Maybe she was more than a little upset.''

Elena continued shaking her head. ''I don't think she'd cut out on a job, no matter how upset she was.'' She went on tiptoe to peer over his shoulder. ''Maybe I should go track her down.''

Griffin set down his glass. ''Let me,'' he offered.

She narrowed her eyes. ''If you're why she's MIA in the first place—''

''Then I should be the one to make things right.''

Elena grimaced. ''Why do I have a bad feeling about this?''

''I do, too,'' he admitted, already moving away. ''Find Logan, will you? Tell him I'm heading through the woods to Annie's.''

Griffin discovered half her shoe on the gravel path near her place. He squeezed it in his palm, trying to control the sharp anxiety growing in his gut. It was just Annie tossing clothes again, he tried telling himself.

Then he heard her voice, coming from around the corner of the cottage. ''I'm sure you didn't want to hurt that bank teller. And you wouldn't really hurt me, would you Joey?''

Hurt her? A tangle of emotion seized Griffin. Dread, anxiety, more dread. His mind whirled. The bank teller. Joey. Joey was the bank robber?

Get control, he commanded himself. *Control.* Rushing in could put Annie in danger.

Joey had a weaselly voice that matched his weaselly face. ''I might hurt you,'' he said.

He might! Griffin froze, again fighting back that rash impulse to act immediately.

As Annie started talking again, Griffin moved swiftly toward the corner of the cottage. "Not me, Joey. You don't want to hurt *me,* right?" Her voice was breathless but not desperate. "Wasn't I the one who taught you to tie your shoes?"

"The rabbit through the hole three times," Joey said. "But that's how you recognized me, right?"

Griffin dared a look around the corner of the building. Annie and Joey were standing behind her little red car. Joey's back was half turned, but Annie was facing him. Her eyes flickered and Griffin pulled back. Think, he told himself, think of a way to get her away with the least amount of risk.

"Lots of people triple-tie their shoes, Joey."

"But a lot of people don't rob banks."

"Yeah, well, you're right. That's pretty unique," Annie said.

Joey laughed. "It's exciting. I'm nothing more than the scissors-and-paste monitor at my uncle's dealership, you know, just like kindergarten. I wanted something new. More. And it wasn't that hard, you know. For each robbery, I take a different car from the lot. 'Test drives' I call them. Never the same one twice."

"Clever," Annie said. "But then you left the gun in the car you sold me. Why was that?"

A gun. Griffin suspected she'd pitched her voice louder for his benefit. *The little weasel had a gun!* Rage, scalding and barely controllable, poured into his blood. *Think of Annie. Be careful for Annie.*

"It was a mistake. I thought I left it in a different

car. But thanks to this party, I have it back now." Joey's voice was suddenly angry. "Geesh. You're just like my uncle. Can't a guy make a mistake once in a while?"

At Joey's abrupt mood change, Griffin instinctively moved forward. Annie and the weasel were in the same positions as before, but now she looked afraid. This time Griffin noticed that her stockings were torn and her knees bloody.

Joey had already hurt her.

Some powerful and primal instinct or emotion—protectiveness, possessiveness, pure fury?—overcame Griffin. It took over his mind, his muscles. One minute he was trying to use his head to rescue Annie and the next his world went from color to black-and-white.

And in the minute following that, he was standing over the fallen body of a stunned-looking Joey Delvecchio. Annie's shoe was lying nearby and Griffin held the gun.

He trained it on the weasel. "Don't move." He didn't recognize his own voice. "Are you all right, Annie?"

Before she could answer, Logan called cheerfully from the other side of the cottage. "Annie? Griffin? Come out, come out wherever you are! We're looking for shrimps."

Griffin yelled back. "Call the police, bro. No shrimps, but we caught ourselves a weasel."

Chapter Fourteen

Annie sat on a leather couch in the Chases' library. Her arms were shoved through Griffin's white dinner jacket and she sipped from a bottomless champagne glass. Bottomless, because Logan was plying everyone with the stuff pouring out of the fountain set up for the anniversary celebration.

"Gotta drink it before it goes flat!" he kept saying, then ducking onto the veranda outside the library doors to refill Elena's glass or her glass, or his father's or mother's.

Elena slumped in the opposite corner of the couch and handed her empty glass to Logan. "No more for me. I can't feel my tongue."

Annie didn't feel anything. Not shock, not astonishment, not even a glimmer of surprise. She glanced at Mrs. Chase, ensconced in her wing chair. She appeared as numb as Annie. "I'm so sorry the party was disrupted," she said to the older woman.

Mrs. Chase, as always, smiled serenely. "Maybe it will be easier for Jonathon to remember our anniversary date now," she said.

Logan slid a full champagne flute into his mother's empty hand. "Sirens and police officers do have a way of sharpening one's focus."

Mr. Chase was rolling a billiard cue in his hand. "March twenty-third. I'm perfectly aware of the date."

The police had come and gone. They'd questioned Annie, and she suspected there would be a lot more questions, but Griffin had stepped in—once again identifying himself as her attorney—and the police had agreed to schedule a longer interview for another day.

As it was, they seemed pretty happy with having possession of the gun. Plus, once Joey was caught he seemed eager to take credit for all the excitement he'd recently brought to the community.

She had an idea his confrontation with Griffin had made him rethink just how many more thrills his life needed. Someone throwing a shoe at your head then slamming you into the ground was bound to alter your perspective. Being at the wrong end of a gun hadn't seemed to float his boat either. Like Annie, Joey was probably regretting the impulse to change his life.

The door to the library opened and Griffin came into the room carrying a plastic box. Annie looked away. He'd been escorting the police out, but now that he was back, it was time for her to go home. The college crew had done a masterful job of storing away the leftover food and Annie figured she could sort through any last details some time later.

Some time when she wouldn't have to be near Griffin's tense watchfulness.

She shrugged out of his coat then made to stand.

"Sit down," Griffin ordered.

Annie pretended she hadn't heard him and came to her feet, a little awkwardly maybe, with only the one shoe. "This may not sound quite right at the moment, but I do wish you a happy anniversary, Mr. and Mrs. Chase."

"Sit *down,* Annie." Griffin dropped the plastic box he held onto the couch beside her. "I need to clean your cuts."

Her gaze followed his. Oh. There were scrapes on her knees, she remembered now, from when she fell on the gravel. "I don't even feel them."

"They need to be cleaned," he insisted.

Annie swallowed. She couldn't stand the idea of him touching her. "Elena can do it."

"I'm sorry, but Elena has had too much champagne," her friend said from her slumped position at the other end of the couch.

"Too much champagne?" Logan strolled forward, wearing a sly little grin. "I think I heard someone call my name."

Elena rolled her eyes. "Did I say Double-crosser? Stander-upper?"

Logan ignored her insults and put his hand above her elbow, hauling her up. "Let's go, girl."

"I'm a *woman,*" Elena grumbled.

"That's what I thought ten years ago," Logan muttered. "Believe me, I don't want to make the same mistake twice." He pulled her from the room.

"Well," said Mrs. Chase, her voice unruffled. "I think I'll go find some coffee."

Annie took a step forward. "I can—"

"Jonathon will help me, won't you, dear?" Mrs. Chase asked, glancing over her shoulder at her husband.

He blinked. "I suppose I will," he said, then followed her out.

"Sit," Griffin said one more time.

His hand came out, and Annie dropped down to the couch. Anything to avoid his touch. She reached for the first-aid box. "I can take care of this myself."

As if she hadn't spoken, he hunkered down at her feet. He gently took one ankle in his hands. Annie stiffened, ordering herself not to tremble.

Straightening her knee, he bent his head over her leg, as if inspecting the scrapes. "Hell, Annie," he whispered hoarsely.

He set her foot on the carpet and rushed to stand, turning his back to her. Shoving his hands in his pockets, he groaned.

Annie swallowed. "What's the matter?"

"I'm a selfish bastard," he said.

"No," she answered automatically.

He let out a short laugh. "I can't remember what happened out there, you know."

Her eyebrows rose. "By the cottage?"

He nodded.

"You did seem a little sketchy on the details when you talked to the police." There'd been a big hole in his story between when he'd heard her warning him about the gun to the point where he was holding it on Joey himself.

"I lost it."

His male shorthand was impossible to follow. "It?"

His back still turned, one hand came out of his pocket and he made an impatient gesture. "My control. My focus. I don't know. Maybe my mind."

"That's understandable."

He whipped around to face her, his blue eyes hard. "Is it? It never happened to me before. I'm always focused. You could have been hurt."

"But I wasn't," she pointed out reasonably, unsure what was driving his mood.

"You don't understand," he said hoarsely, dropping back down at her feet. "What I did.... It wasn't a conscious decision, a conscious choice. I just...acted. I had to."

Annie couldn't help herself from reaching out and touching his hair. Her fingers just brushed the soft stuff. "Is that the selfish part?"

He looked up, caught her hand, brought it to his lips. He kissed her fingertips and the light sensation skittered up her arm like the trail of a butterfly. Annie closed her eyes. Even if he couldn't love her, it didn't change how she felt about him.

Pain pierced her heart, and Annie wished futilely for that numbness back. "Oh, Griffin," she heard herself whisper.

"Oh, Annie."

For a second she thought he sounded as heartbroken as she. *But of course he couldn't be,* she thought. *He wasn't.*

"I...wish we could go back. Do things differently," he said, still holding her hand.

"Funny you should mention that." She smiled a little. "Right before I ran into Joey I was wishing the very same thing. I think I like staying behind the trees and in the corners a lot better than whatever you call what I've been doing lately."

"Falling in love?"

Annie looked away.

"You regret falling in love with me?"

She didn't know. How could she? How could she decide whether the risks were worth it when there'd been heaven and there'd been heartbreak?

Both sides of life, a little voice inside her whispered. *That's what really living is all about.* No pain, no gain. No guts, no glory. Clichés were clichés sometimes because they were so true.

"Do you, Annie?" Griffin took her chin in his hand and forced her to look at him. "Do you regret falling in love with me?"

What was the point of lying to herself? Of lying to him? She dumbly shook her head.

His fingers tightened on her face. "Okay." He let go of her, stood. "Okay," he said again. "But you might. This is where the selfish part comes in."

Puzzled, she looked up at him. "Blame it on the champagne if you want, but this Y-chromosome code of yours is starting to make my head spin. You might want to give me the uncondensed version."

He ran his palm down his face, then he looked at her, his gaze slamming into her with an intensity she'd only seen in him once before. "I want you, Annie."

Her heart started pounding and her pulse began throbbing. Heat washed over her. "I…" She had no idea what to say. She couldn't keep sharing his bed without shredding her heart.

"Forever, Annie. I want you forever."

She blinked.

He began pacing on the carpet in front of her. "It was all so lucid to me in that moment. My mind blanked out, I had no idea what my body was doing, but somewhere else inside me the situation was perfectly clear. I have to have you."

Her heartbeat slipped into higher gear. "I—I think you're doing that male code thing again."

He stopped in front of her. "You have to know what you're getting into with me. I get wrapped up in my work. I'm distant. I don't feel intensely. That's what I've been told. But I don't believe any more that I can't commit to someone. To you. I told you earlier today that I wouldn't because I was afraid I'd hurt you. But hell, Annie, I think I've always been afraid I'd get hurt, too."

His chest was heaving with his harsh breaths and his eyes were so blue Annie thought they might burn her. "I'm sorry I can't love you. But I feel…possessive of you, Annie. Protective. Something. I feel something so damn bad that I'll risk hurt because I don't want ever to let you go."

Annie blinked again, then gave a quick glance around, looking for the fairy godmother she needed to thank. Certainly there was magic in the room, sparkling like stardust in the air. She let out a long breath of air. "Let me get this straight. You don't love me, but you want me forever?"

He nodded, the blue heat in his eyes not abating.

"You want to protect me?"

He nodded again.

"Kind of like you've been doing lately? Not so tied up in the company, but instead being with me, taking time from work to go places with me, eating with me…sleeping with me?"

He took his own breath. "That's what I want," he confessed, as if it was a sin.

"But the bank robber's been caught."

His hand moved impatiently. "Not protect you from danger, necessarily. Just…I don't know. Partner you."

He wanted to partner her. Somewhere there was a ballroom with musicians and royal guests. A glittering gown made by mice and a crown with her name on it. There just had to be. "Because of this intense feeling you have?"

He hunkered down in front of her, and gathered her hands in his. She thought he was trembling. "I don't know what else to call it, Annie. But yeah, that's the gist of it."

He didn't know what else to call it. Annie closed her eyes. Griffin wasn't a character in a fairy tale or a fantasy. Any lingering insecurity vanished as she realized that only a real man could be shaking like this. Only a real man could be this dumb. "That's all right. You don't have to give it a name," Annie said, leaning forward to kiss him. It was enough that *she* knew what it was.

His lips were warm and substantial and the shudder

that ran through him was anything but imagined. "You just have to give me the rest of your life," she said.

His arm around Annie, Griffin paused at the entry to the banquet room of the restaurant where his parents were hosting the rehearsal dinner for their wedding. The long table was nearly full, signalling that he and Annie were among the last to arrive. Due to the church's busy schedule, they were eating first and rehearsing later and it looked like everyone was waiting for them.

He squeezed her waist. "You're the one who has to apologize. I've been ready for hours."

She lifted on tiptoe to kiss his cheek. "I know."

"Days," he continued against her ear. "Months. Years."

"Spare me." Annie rolled her eyes. "You didn't give me the time of day years ago and we've only been engaged less than two months."

"It seems longer." It seemed too long.

Annie grinned at him, her single dimple digging deep in her cheek. "That's just because you got stuck with all the wedding details."

True. Annie's second brush with danger had sounded the same wake-up call to Annie's mother that it had to him. She had looked hard at her life, and then, convinced Griffin was going to take good care of Annie in Strawberry Bay, Natalie Smith had moved to her sister's in San Diego. With her mother a few hours away and Annie swamped with catering jobs, Griffin had taken time off from work to take charge of all the nuptial details that nobody else wanted. There were an astonishing number of that kind of details, he'd discovered.

"It's going to be a beautiful day," he said.

Annie leaned into him. "No matter what the weather is."

"I ordered sunshine." Exactly what finding Annie—or maybe finally *seeing* her—had brought into his life. He smiled. "And I have a surprise for you tonight."

"Oh?"

He smiled again. She had no idea. "Yep. I'm going to prove to you how smart I am, just as soon as you sit down."

Her brows came together. "Smart? Of course I think you're smart. Are you or are you not the vice-president of Chase Electronics?"

As if that alone would ever have truly satisfied him. He smiled as he led her to their empty chairs in the center of the long table. "Sit down, sweetheart."

Annie gave her apologies to the guests for being late. A waiter poured champagne. Griffin tapped a fork against his water glass to get the guests' attention.

"Now to show you how smart I am," he murmured to Annie. He raised his voice. "I want to give everyone a chance to ooh and aah at once." From his jacket pocket, he slipped a small box.

He looked at Annie. Funny, how such a simple thing could make his hands shake. "I know you said you didn't want an engagement ring, but I couldn't resist getting you something special..." He flipped open the top of the box.

Annie gasped. Everyone else oohed and aahed appropriately. It was a ring, not an engagement ring exactly, but one that he hoped would say all he should have months ago. It was a clear sparkling diamond set in the shape of a heart.

He took the ring out of the box, his fingers so stiff they fumbled. The piece of jewelry fell to the tablecloth and Annie retrieved it for him. Tears in her eyes, she looked at him. "You *are* smart," she said. "I love it."

His heart slammed against his chest. "Read the inscription," he said hoarsely.

Annie gave him a curious look, then obediently tilted the ring to read what was carved inside. She stilled. Then a single tear spilled down her cheek.

His gut clenched. Thank God he'd given it to her in public. She made him want to cry himself, or better yet, make love to her. They hadn't been to bed together since the night of his parents' anniversary party and their engagement—one of them had had the dumb idea of waiting until the wedding—and he wanted her so damn badly right now. Tomorrow night, he wouldn't have a prayer of controlling his desire, but he didn't care.

She looked at him. "You...?" she whispered.

He nodded. "I told you I was smart. I love you, Annie." He took the ring from her. It felt warm in his hand and it fitted her finger perfectly. "It just took me a while to give my feelings a name."

He'd been so convinced that his focus on the family company meant he couldn't love. But it had only taken finding someone, the right someone, *to* love. It had taken finding Annie to know that love and marriage could be different for him than for his father.

Annie's eyes closed. He bent to kiss her, tender and gentle because his love for her was so damn powerful, so damn deep. The hand wearing the heart ring came up and stroked his hair. He thought she was trembling now, too.

"I'm so glad I stopped hiding," Annie whispered.

"Or else I wouldn't have found the one woman I was waiting for," Griffin whispered back.

They kissed again. Griffin might never have lifted his head unless the chair beside his hadn't suddenly scraped out and a big body fallen into its seat.

"Bro, Annie," said Logan breathlessly. "Sorry I'm late. I had a flat." He ran his hands through his hair. "Geez. It's been a hell of a day."

Griffin didn't let go of Annie's hands as he cleared his throat. "Did you...did you come alone?"

"Of course I came alone," Logan answered. "I told you I wasn't bringing a date tonight."

Griffin looked at Annie, his eyebrows raised. Annie looked back at him. She shook her head. "I don't think I love you that much. He's your brother. You're going to have to remind him."

Logan didn't move his head, but his eyes swiveled toward them. "Remind me of what?" he asked warily.

Griffin ran his tongue over his teeth. He chugged his glass of champagne. He squeezed Annie's fingers for moral support. "You were supposed to pick up Elena," he said gently. "Remember?"

Logan's entire body froze. Griffin wondered if he was even breathing. His voice sounded funny, too. Strained. Upset. "Are you telling me I stood her up again?"

But he had already vaulted out of his chair and was running for the door.

Griffin looked at Annie.

Annie looked at Griffin.

"Again?" they said together.

After a moment, Annie shrugged. "You wised up. Perhaps there's hope."

"Oh, yeah." Griffin grinned down at his wife-to-be, the woman he adored, because she made him so stupidly happy. "There's always hope."

Hadn't he given up on love and marriage once upon a time? But Annie had made him believe again.

*   *   *   *   *

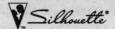
SPECIAL EDITION™
is delighted to present

The
Stockwells
of Texas

Available January–May 2001

Where family secrets, scandalous pasts and unexpected love wreak havoc on the lives of the infamous Stockwells of Texas!

THE TYCOON'S INSTANT DAUGHTER
by Christine Rimmer
(SE #1369) on sale January 2001

SEVEN MONTHS AND COUNTING...
by Myrna Temte
(SE #1375) on sale February 2001

HER UNFORGETTABLE FIANCÉ
by Allison Leigh
(SE #1381) on sale March 2001

THE MILLIONAIRE AND THE MOM
by Patricia Kay
(SE #1387) on sale April 2001

THE CATTLEMAN AND THE VIRGIN HEIRESS
by Jackie Merritt
(SE #1393) on sale May 2001

Available at your favorite retail outlet.

Silhouette®
Where love comes alive™

Visit Silhouette at www.eHarlequin.com   SSESOT

Silhouette Books and
award-winning, bestselling author

LINDSAY McKENNA

are proud to present

MORGAN'S MERCENARIES:
IN THE BEGINNING...

These first stories

HEART OF THE WOLF
THE ROGUE
COMMANDO

introduce Morgan Trayhern's *Perseus Team*—
brave men and bold women who travel
the world righting wrongs, saving lives...
and resisting love to their utmost.
They get the mission done—but rarely escape
with their hearts intact!

*Don't miss these exciting stories available in April 2001—
wherever Silhouette titles are sold.*

Silhouette®

™ *Where love comes alive*™

BR3MM

Award-winning, bestselling authors

Christine Rimmer
& Laurie Paige

are known for their heartwarming, emotional stories of
family, children and the connections that grow between
couples. Here are two compelling stories about
marriages of convenience....

DOUBLE DARE
They'd known each other forever and Casey and Joanna
married to keep custody of his nephew. But sharing a life, a
family...a *bed*...wasn't like anything they'd ever expected....

MOLLY DARLING
He knew his tiny daughter needed a mother—and that
Molly would shower Lass with tender care. But what
happened when Sam realized he wanted Molly's love,
tenderness and *passion* for himself?

Come see how
Convenient Vows
become anything but
convenient in May 2001.

Available wherever Silhouette books are sold!